W9-CEK-542

Vendetta

Diary of a kingpin's daughter...

By

Lenaise Meyeil

Diary of a Kingpin's Daughter

The sale of this book without its cover is unauthorized. If you purchased this book without a cover, you should be aware that it was reported to the publisher as "unsold and destroyed". Neither the author nor the publisher has received payment for the sale of this stripped book.

This book is a work of fiction. Names, characters, places, and incidents are results of the author's imagination or are used fictitiously. Any resemblance to locations, actual events or persons, living or dead is entirely coincidental.

Precioustymes Entertainment
229 Governors Place, #138
Bear, DE 19701
www.precioustymes.com
www.myspace.com/precioustymesent

Library of Congress Control Number: 2007909772
ISBN# 0-9776507-7-4
       978-0-9776507-7-4
Editor: Laketa Lewis
Proofreader: Lorna
Female Photographer: Doss Tidwell
Cover models: Stiletto Princess & Craig of Phat Cuts Barbershop – Wilmington, DE
Cover Design/Graphics: Kevin Carr/ocjgraphix.com
Email Lenaise @ lenaisemeyeil@yahoo.com

Copyright © 2006 by Lenaise Meyeil. All rights reserved. No part of this book may be reproduced in any form without permission from the Author, except by reviewers who may quote brief passages to be printed in a newspaper, magazine, or an online literary webpage.

First Trade Paperback Edition Printed April 2008
Printed in United States

By Lenaise Meyeil

Acknowledgements

Jesus said, "In this world you will have trouble. But take heart! I have overcome the world." John 16:33

I have to start this acknowledgement off by saying God is so good to me. I am truly blessed!! He promised to never leave nor forsake me, and to those words I live by. Everyday it gives me the power and courage to continue on the path that my Father has laid out for me. I love you O Lord, my strength. Psalm 18:1

Last time I had at least three pages shouting out and thanking so many...and yet I still managed to forget some, I apologized a thousand times over. One person in particular that was very upset behind that, my good friend and the mother of my first Godchild, Dayveon M. Minnerick, Angie you know the love I have for you is much stronger than a pen could ever reveal. As well as, a deep apology to my dear Uncle Larry.

To my entire family: The~ Williams, Moore, Smith, Blair, Flex, Hewitt and Hodges: you guys have been my biggest supporters from the start. Always believing in me and encouraging me to keep going...you inspire me to do more. To my "Bammow" Catherine Moore, thank you so much for really pushing Stiletto like you did~ knowing how proud of me, you are, drives me to do my best. To my sister, there is no greater love. If nobody else has my back I know you do~ I promise you when I get rich I'm going to take care of you sis...I'll probably owe some cash any way (Lol). Mom Linda Williams, You give me hope, strength and security, you are the true meaning of an Independent woman I do this all for you mommy, and your baby girl is going to take care of you to!!! Nakiya~"mini me", know that you deserve nothing but the best, so except nothing less, wit cha smart mouth ass!. To my brothers, I love you guys so much: Termaine, the twins Deonte and Deandre~ I know you guys will make me so proud one day! Cousin Tanya, you deserve a paragraph from me girl! You have been my constant strength since my move, always reminding me of what's really important, never allowing me to lose focus. Thanks Bitch, do you love it!!! Lol. You to Aunt Daneen!! Candis, Erica, Kim, and Janata, and Khalida, who needs friends when I have cousins like you. To the rest of the fam, just because I didn't mention your name this time does not mean I don't appreciate you. I love it!!!

To my friends: Thanks for being there for me, supporting me and believing in me at all times and never being judgmental~ even when you knew~ that I knew better. Jesus said, "Greater love has no one than his: to lay down one's life for one's friends~ This was written because He knew we would forever be in each others lives: Attorney Lakesha Kintop, Juwania Keys, Crystal Blough (Hey Jurnee Meyeia~Rose, I miss you), Tracy Allen, Nyesha Maddix, LaKesha Johnson Sylvia Massey, and Urmika "MiMi" Branch. We have all done well over a decade together and I look forward to many more. Katrice Young, you and Amaya, you guys were my welcome wagon to Houston (thank you friend & little friend lol). Vanesha "Vernisha" as I would say, I really appreciate your honest feedback, motivation and the support. Lydell one of my best friends, nobody understands the bond we have, the perfect thing about it is, and we don't care! Ms. Chantel Stoval, the image of a woman making moves, I love you~ thanks for keeping it" funky"! Tameka Finely "sister", thanks for simply being you with no "bs" attached. Ms. Marsha Wilson thanks for having my back and working the hell out of stiletto for me. Jeffery Coleman, I still and always will love you baby~til death do us part...I'm still holding on to our pact! (smile) I know at times I may drift but I will never disappear.

I have so many others dear to me that have truly been in my corner it would take many pages to name them all, you know who you are... Thank you all!

To my fabulous publisher~KaShamba Williams-PTE baby! Thanks for your patience with me and your genuine advice. You've really helped me grow as a writer as well as a businesswoman. I really appreciate you and all of your hard work. I'm very proud to be signed with PTE, and still, we rise!! You know I have to say my favorite line "you're the bomb!" Lol. Ms. Heather Covington, thank for all your support, you truly inspire me. And to all the distributors, bookstores, vendors, book clubs, that support PTE. Shout out to all PTE authors – keep it coming. Chi-town is representing though :). Thank you to Laketa Lewis and to Lorna for your contribution.

The entire Milwaukee, Wisconsin (yes black people live there) lol~ you guys really have shown me so much love & support. The love you guys gave Stiletto 101 was overwhelming. I can't thank you enough!! V100 FM, Urban

Diary of a Kingpin's Daughter

connection bookstore, Playmakers (Jim Callie, Ms. Do nothing~ Jesten McCord, Milwaukee Journal Sentinel News paper, -Leonard Sykes, Channel 10, and John Moore + Many others. I love my city

Special shout out to Joel Rhodes, author of "Victim of the Ghetto", because of you I shine brighter on the inside~ "Pinky and the Brain" all day cuzo!! We are going to take over the world!!

I'd also like to give a big thanks to Houston, TX, the place I now call home: African Imports Book store: Obie, i10media-David Anderson, Indmix: Ikem you've shown me love from my first intro to Houston's nightlife, Houston Honeyz, Orbitz.com, All theparties.com, CJ, Wiley and Quest, you guys really help put me on the map with the fab pictures and promo! John Aaron for always being there when I needed you. L.O.W.~ the short time we were acquainted has left a lasting impression on my life. Thanks for your constant reminder that "everything is fine"~ May God continue to bless you, you've taught me what it truly means to humble one-self. Thanks for everything; I mean that! Tummy you were and always will be the realest!

If God is for me; than who can be against me! Romans 8:13

HOLLA AT CHA GURL
   LENAISE MEYEIL aka The Stiletto Princess

This book is
Dedicated to
"My American Gangster"
My father,
Otis Moore Jr.
7-26-60/6-9-03
(My Personal Angel)

Vendetta

Diary of a kingpin's daughter...

By

Lenaise Meyeil

Diary of a Kingpin's Daughter

Dear Diary,

This may be my last time confiding in you - my only unbiased friend - the only thing he can't turn against me. And to think, he was the one that told me writing would be good therapy for me. I know my secrets to you are starting to begin the same with each page, but he hit me again!! I thought last time would be the last time. He promised. Only this one wasn't as bad, I've had worse. I'm really starting to feel like I'm going insane. I have been having all these crazy thoughts about killing myself just to escape this misery thinking this would be my only peaceful way out. I can't believe I've allowed him in my head that much to be suicidal. OMG! I loved this man so much that now I despise him. I just wish he would die or go to jail for life. I know that sounds harsh, but that is the only way he will leave me alone or I can rid my life of him; get him out of my system. I feel like there is no other way out. I've damn near tried everything and with each attempt things get worse. I can't believe my life has come to this. I'm so ashamed. I let this man strip me of my pride, my self-esteem, and my name. My father would be so embarrassed of me if he were still breathing. Naw, fuck that. If my father were still alive, none of this would be happening. Does this nigga know who I am? I think he forgot I am the daughter of the one, and only, legendary,

John Otis Carter aka JO, nigga! He worshiped the ground my father walked on. Yeah and my dad put him on, made him the nigga he is today. Now he wants to act as if he's the fucking King of New York or some damn body. I don't know what the hell I'm gonna do to hide my black eye this time. Oh, and my left wrist is sprained too... bastard! I'm really starting to think this man is repulsed by me. Whatever hidden animosity he had for my father, he is taking it out on me. Every time he beats me, he says, "Call your daddy for help now, bitch!" When I look into his dark eyes, all I see is hate and coldness; no more love. This is the same man that asked my father for my hand in marriage and promised to take care of me and love me till death do us part. The same man that begged me to have his baby and to be his wife. The same man that I've loved since I was 15-years-old! I just don't understand where I went wrong. I can't take this shit anymore!

GOD, please forgive me. I no longer feel protected and secure with the life that I have been dealt. I am afraid and without options. I pray that I escape this hell on earth forever. Amen.

It's ya gurl,
Chloe Baguette Carter-Wright

A legend is made

Last of a dying thorough-breed... John Otis was born to a poverty stricken family, so it wasn't surprising when the only son of a low budget mechanic and homemaker decided to step up and be the man his father wasn't. Born John Otis Carter, known to the streets JO, he started off as a small-time peddler with a charming personality. He was a tall handsome man, with an athletic build, smooth flawless skin, and perfect white teeth with the complexion of an Arab. He could stare a nun out of her panties with his big, brown, shiny eyes, complimented with his thick, silky eyebrows. He had looks, charm, game, and a jumping name in the streets. His existence was so dominating; his scent introduced him in every room. Not an ordinary hood nigga, JO could jump from thug to Maury loafers and a tailor made suit in one shower.

Hand-picked by a local supplier that had connections with the areas mob relatives named The Mangialardi's (also known as Mangialardi La Familia), JO was watched over the course of a year, and got off more work (dope) than the cats buying by the kilos. His need to re-up came so hurriedly that he had the bosses in awe of his manhandle. He was a student of the streets way before he tried his hand at it. It's almost like he premeditated it, earned a degree, continued, and then mastered the game like a chess proficient. JO was an intellectual without high levels of education. Even as a self taught student, he became fluent in Spanish.

Eventually the Mangialardi's started to front JO kilos of cocaine at a time, automatically boosting his rank to the crown. With loyalty, he aced the test with an A+ and was soon known as one of the highest class drug dealers in the city. In less than a year, he went from the new kid on the block to owning every drug house on the block. He became an important aspect to La Familia, so ordered protection was there during the handling of product and large sums of cash.

Although JO wasn't gang affiliated, he had guaranteed protection from one of the city's most feared gangs, the Gangster Disciples. This caused many to turn to him for direction, support, and leadership. Although, it also caused envy amongst those that he wouldn't fuck with. Not everyone was enthused and ready to bow down to him.

What started off as a neighborhood operation, expanded into a citywide drug trafficking business. He was modest enough to share his newfound fame with his best friend, Monte "Money Green" Wright, and a few other qualified links. Straight out of high school to the pros; JO was a made man. He was the official chief of his project residence, Wentworth Gardens, where he grew up. The Mangialardi's assured him an endless supply of cocaine and in return, he made them hefty revenue. The police force was never an issue with JO paying off the captain of law enforcement - $10,000 monthly to divert officials from his turf. Competition was never an issue since part of the Po-Po's job was to do away with rival hustlers. That meant busting competition on bogus charges or arranging vanishings.

Life seemed all too perfect for one of the cities largest crime bosses. To many, he seemed invincible. God made no man in flesh perfect; even the ghetto prince had flaws. JO's weakness was the bitches. Beautiful females that was at least 16 and over. The weak-willed imperfection of his was definitely his fixation with younger girls and his only rule was that he didn't tamper with virgins. Women and young girls swarmed around him and if they were ripe and sexing, he was accepting. Enough said. It was said that he fathered many children, other than Chloe, but it was never confirmed.

JO's most regretful victim happened to be his best friend's wife, Tina and also, best friend to his high school sweetheart and his soon to be wife, Kim.

Kim was slightly older than him, standing at an even 5'9" and had sexy bow-legs. JO always adored how she was so tall, but still had to look up to him for direct eye contact him.

Diary of a Kingpin's Daughter

Years into their relationship, the day John Otis found out Kim was pregnant, was the same day they married.

"I always said the woman I fell in love with that loved me equal in yolk, would be the mother of my children and my wife. Kim let's do this," he said, in his way of proposing to her.

It was that day JO opened completely up to her, introducing her to the good life where money was supposed to solve all their problems. Still, he continued on with his infidelity. The affair with Tina painstakingly ended in a heartbreaking suicide and it wasn't JO that died *that* night.

There were a few outcasts that were overcome with extreme envy, including his best friend's wife and mistress, Tina before she decided to take her life. She was determined to destroy Kim's fairytale life with her lover, especially since she felt like Kim duped her of earning the title of Mrs. John Otis Carter. She often bluffed to expose their secret affair, hoping he would leave Kim. Even asking JO to relocate her to another city and state so they could have real time alone if only for a few days out of the month. Although, it never happened the way she envisioned causing her obsession to be a permanent fixture in his life, her one and only goal. JO had no other choice, but to cut her off since Tina was out of control.

JO's extra martial affairs didn't stop at Tina. He was infamous for shoving hush money to his side pieces, so every female leaped at his provoke. Kim endured countless nights of prank calls, anonymous letters, and many crude remarks that she wasn't the only woman with JO's child. Even with that drama Kim had no intentions of allowing any gossip or infidelity ruin her comfy lifestyle. She felt like regardless of his crooked manners outside of the house, his heart and true feel for affection was at home with her and the princess she gave birth to, Chloe Baguette Carter.

A Princess is born

The day princess Chloe was born, if you lived in the hood around the Robert Taylor Project Homes all the way through Wentworth Gardens, you might have thought the President was due to visit. JO shut down blocks and had a huge ass block party for the hood. Everyone had to rejoice the birth of his first-born child; his baby girl, Chloe. He even gave his workers the day off. All susceptible, he probably let the fiends smoke a rock on him that day too. He was that elated about the birth of his baby girl.

From the very beginning, Chloe was taught quality, not quantity and to accept nothing less. John Otis even named her Chloe Baguette because he said it suited his little diamond. When she was 5 months and ready to get her ears pierced, he purchased her a lavish pair of 1-carat diamond earring studs. Kim had to beg him to wait for the clearance from the doctor to change the studs in fear of him splitting her tiny earlobes. For Chloe's 1st birthday, she got her first pair of Gucci shoes. Kim even had a Gucci baby carrier with the matching designer diaper bag. Chloe's nursery was decorated by a professional interior decorator with the finest Egyptian fabrics. Spoiled from the very beginning, Chloe was indeed a material girl in the making.

By Lenaise Meyeil

Princess meets the streets

Most of Chloe's life was sheltered from anything labeled as unacceptable. They lived in Orland Park, the suburbs, about 30 minutes from JO's original hood. She attended a private school from pre-school through grade school. John Otis paid well for her to receive the best education with the cities most elite children. The Mayor's son, the daughters of some of the top CEO's of the most prestigious companies in town, and many wealthy trust fund babies. Chloe stomped with the "big wigs" kids.

For high school though, she begged her parents to allow her to go to a public school where the kids were not so snooty and prejudice. In reality, she wanted to have fun and attend school where there were fewer restrictions. Mostly, she felt like she was missing out on something. Kim agreed because she did not want Chloe to be too prissy and unaware of the real world. She used to constantly remind her. "Your daddy and I won't always be here, so you need to learn how to survive without us. It's a cruel world out here princess; a world where bad does exist. So, you need to be both book smart and street smart."

After lots of arguments and convincing, JO hesitantly agreed with Kim's decision to allow

Chloe to use her Aunt Ryan's address to attend public school.

Chloe loved to stay at her Aunt Ryan's house every chance she got. That's because she lived in the hood that JO's empire was built around and would allow the girls to run wild and free. Everybody knew not to fuck with them.

In exchange for attending public school, during her free time, Chloe had to continue activities like piano lessons, ballet, and gymnastics during most weekends. That's why it took her by total surprise when her mother agreed so easily to ask her father about this new transition.

Starting Bloom High School was nothing like Chloe imagined. It was a world within itself and all of the students were grown-ups, stuck in teenage bodies. The girls wore heels to school with outfits fit for the night club scene. All of the boys had cell phones, pagers, and flashy cars. One of them even had a '94 Cadillac on chrome rims and it was still only '93. Chloe loved every bit of this young society called high school. Most of her cousins went to Bloom High School so being there was a comfort zone for her. Who her father was alone guaranteed her a place in the in-crowd and the girl to associate with.

In school with the little sub-cliques trying to recruit her, the crew that Chloe decided to join was the "*Untouchables*". The original members were a group of senior girls, who would usually pass on the clique's name in their senior wills. As a tradition, the seniors would select protégés for the following year.

Although Chloe was a freshman, she was an honorary member, and along with her, was her favorite cousin Candice aka "Squeak" Sholes. Squeak is Ryan's only daughter of three boys. Hardly anyone ever saw the boys, especially since they were always in and out of juvi' for petty crimes. If they could have stayed out of jail long enough, they would have had the empire practically handed to them. Although, JO always said they were too ignorant to understand. Growing up the only girl in the house explains why Squeak was such a tomboy. She'd been given the name Squeak because of her high-pitched baby like voice. She stood about 5'6" at 16-years-old with the perfect hourglass shape. She was slim in the waist and pretty in the face, but would go toe-to-toe with a boy if she had to. Her looks fit the prissy chick's profile, but her actions were the complete opposite. The only way Chloe was accepting a membership was if her cousin could be accepted as well; they were a package deal. For Squeak, it didn't really matter if she joined or not; she was just happy to have Chloe rolling in school with her. With or without those prissy chicks, Chloe had status. The Untouchable needed her more than she needed them. Especially since all of their fathers worked for JO.

Bionca, Taylor, and Cashay were the first official inheritress of the crew. Bionca was bi-racial (Hispanic and Black) with a cappuccino complexion, had hair like a Hawaiian island girl and most of all bilingual, and by far the most mature of the clique. She had full lips and wide hips and she was the crew's sex expert and daughter of Juan, a Lieutenant in JO's army. Taylor, the black version of Marilyn Monroe, was a total vintage lover. She was dark skin with coco brown eyes that matched her hair, which sat chin length to shape her round face that she wore in tight Monroe curls. She was the most feminine of the crew, and she was the crew's etiquette expert. Her father Lando was another Lieutenant in JO's until his untimely fatal motorcycle accident. Lastly, describing Cashay is like describing a twin to Chloe. They were certainly two of a kind; others often called them twins in school. Cashay, or "Cassay" as they called her, had long, pretty legs like a model, long, thick hair that accented her small narrow face, and eyes like an Asian. She was the crew's boy expert. She kept everyone up on who drove what, what kind of money they had, who they worked for, word on what the dick was like, and who they were fucking. She was the daughter of Monte "Money Green" Wright, JO's best friend. Like Chloe, Cashay was also a daddy's girl. The only difference between them was that Chloe had her mother in her life. Years had gone by since Tina committed suicide.

Out of them all, Chloe stood out the most with beauty, body and status. Standing at a faultless 5'7, complexion the color of corn mill, long legs, slanted eyes, with a petite frame, and big breasts, she was the crew's fashion expert. She kept them up on the latest and hottest gear, which made them trendsetters. Along with tag-along Squeak as the strong arm, they were the most admired and hated collection of females in Bloom High School, the "*Untouchables*".

Their fathers loved the fact that their little dime pieces were in the same pack. Every day, JO would have to drive Chloe across town to school. After a while, he grew tired of it, so he paid Money Green's 18-year-old son, Brezell, b.k.a "Breezy", an upcoming soldier to pick her up every morning along with Cashay, his younger sister. It was this union that caused Chloe heaven and hell. Breezy was tall like a ball player with a solid body from lifting weights and he had the smoothest suntan skin without the sun. Like JO, Breezy was attractive and easy on the eyes for the young ladies unlike his father.

From Chloe begging all the time to drive, eventually, Brezell began to teach Chloe how to drive everyday after school as long as she promised not to tell her father.

Many days on the way to school, Chloe fantasized and would stare in awe from the back seat, imagining Breezy's sexy full lips pressed against her body. He caught her stares and one

By Lenaise Meyeil
21

day, made an advance by winking back at her; instantly her heart melted. The entire day in school she thought about Brezell and couldn't wait until the driving lesson after school that day to see him again. Her hormones were petitioning and she had to let him know how she felt about him.

Since Cashay and Chloe had certainly become best friends, Chloe decided to confide the fact she was obsessing over her older brother. She called Cashay as soon as she got home, she would have blushed to death if she told her in person.

"Hey Cassy, what's good?" Chloe blurted, practicing the slang she picked up from school. Her answer to the question was the celebration of her new item; no words could be made out because she was so ecstatic. "What?" Chloe shouted irritated.

"Girl, Monte bought me a car!" she said excitedly, referring to her father. "A mu-tha-fucking car!" Without taking a breath she recapped her car. "I got a drop-top Audi with a wood-grain steering wheel, a 5-disk CD changer, an alarm, and some 16"gold rims!"

"What! Are you serious? Now that's what's up!" Chloe shouted back thrilled for her. Part of her was disappointed because she wanted to continue to ride with Brezell and the other half was happy because now the girls could really hit the streets full time on their own. No more having to be picked up and dropped off for every event. Cashay was the first out of the circle to get a car, so she was now the reserved driver.

"Girl, click over and call Tay on the three-way so we can tell her we got a car!"

That's another reason Cashay was Chloe's favorite, she was the only person that really lived by, "If you my people and I got it, you got it." She was so selfless when it came to those she loved and everyone appreciated that about her. She might have also been the only person that would give you her last. She was surely Chloe's best confidant.

"Wuz up?" Taylor replied as soon as she picked up the phone.

Like a duet, Cashay and Chloe blurted, "Hey girl!"

"Tell her... Chloe... tell her!" Cashay squeaked, like a kid on Christmas.

"Girl, Money bought Cashay a car so we on wheels now."

"What the fuck! You lying, hold on let me call B." Taylor clicked over and called Bionca to let her in on the good news. Bionca in turn joined Squeak in on the conversation and like a singing group, they we were all on the phone chiming.

"Bitches, where we goin' ta'night?" Squeak said in her soprano tone.

Bionca spoke up first, "Mike Jones' new movie *The American Dream* is coming out tonight and y'all know all the up and comings will be there." She reminded them referring to all the new hustlers on the rise.

Right away, Chloe made the plans official because she knew Brezell would be there. "That's all it is than girls, it's on! Cashay what's the deal?"

"That's what's up than! Everybody be ready by 8'clock p.m. Dress to impress, and be ready to catch something hot," Cashay answered, acknowledging the ghetto celebs that could possibly be at the debut. "Oh yeah, Brezell got a new Escalade, but y'all will see young Breezy shine tonight 'cause you know my fine ass bro gonna be there."

"For real?" The entire group said on cue. They all burst out laughing because they were getting so close, they were really starting to talk alike and think alike.

Chloe wanted to quiz Cashay so badly, but didn't want to give up her crush to everybody at once.

The conference call was ended as everyone started preparing for the night. Chloe ran straight to her mom's room to tell her Cashay's good news and to tell her, her plans for the evening.

"Just make sure you're responsible. Hint. Hint." Kim addressed. She wanted her princess to be sociable, but she also wanted her to be safe. JO on the other hand, didn't want his daughter victim to the streets. He felt like he could forever protect his princess from the ills of the streets.

"Baguette, I got a Ph.D. in *streetology*. That means I got these muthafuckas on lock. I betta not hear one foul ass thing about you, you heard that?"

"Yes, daddy. Now how do I look?" Chloe posed side to side showing off her slim jeans that fit every curve on her body.

"Like the beautiful gem you are. Here, take this lil' roll and have a good time with your friends."

That night at the movies the only chance Chloe had to get at Brezell was full of previews. The entire night he sped around the parking lot in his new Escalade with silver 26" rims. Chloe wasn't worried though, since she would have her chance soon enough because Brezell finally made rank in her father's army. He would be within arms reach from now on, so she wouldn't have to try as hard. However, it wasn't as easy as she thought. Brezell was about paper chasing, not Chloe chasing. This was one of many nights that Chloe would have a difficult time trying to get Brezell to give her the immediate attention she desired.

It wasn't until the end of her sophomore year that she finally had him cornered. Three of her girls, Bionca, Taylor, and Cashay were graduating and to celebrate, Money Green was throwing them a huge pool party. Everybody who was somebody would be there, especially, those in John Otis' camp. This was the ultimate chance for Chloe to make her move on Brezell. The day before the party, Kim, Squeak, and Chloe went on Michigan Street, which was best known as Designer Blvd., to find swim wear. Kim was a firm believer in quality, so Chloe knew there was no price limit on what swimsuit they chose. It took Chloe damn near the entire day to find one bathing suit that screamed *one hot item*. Squeak's taste wasn't as extravagant; she was the easy-to-please kind so she chose a one-piece Ralph Lauren swimsuit with the matching flip flops and a large Polo beach towel and bag. The last store before Kim really started to show her irritation for Chloe's indecisiveness was where Chloe finally found the suit to die for. She choose a very high priced, two-piece, plaid Christian Dior bikini set with the thong sandals to match and a sheer spaghetti strap Dior dress to go over it. When John Otis got wind of what she chose, he and her mother both agreed they created a high-maintenance monster. Chloe couldn't wait to let Brezell see how her stylish threads held her tender 34 D-cups. After that, he would wish those were his hands instead of the bikini top. She was planning to rep and flirt like it was her given name.

JO and Juan drove Chloe and Bionca to the pool party. The entire time, JO lectured Chloe on her choice of the 2-piece; he hadn't realized how much his little pumpkin had sprouted.

"JO you know Chloe's nickname is going to change tonight, right?" Juan uttered to him.

JO in turn, turned to him baffled, "What the fuck are you talkin' 'bout Juan?"

"Man, no disrespect, but your princess is gonna be the Queen Bee tonight with that. How you gonna stop those young boys from gettin' at her?"

JO immediately grew angry. "That was exactly my point. I told Kim about letting that girl wear shit like that. Baguette, you gotta cover up with that thing?"

"Yes, daddy," she giggled, and smiled at Bionca.

Once they arrived, Chloe and Bionca flew out the car inside the pool party before John Otis changed his mind.

Chloe dauntlessly sashayed around the pool in search of Brezell. For some reason, it seemed like Bionca had the same intentions on getting at Brezell as Chloe did. Every time Chloe spotted him, Bionca was in his mix, and from the looks of it he was enjoying her Latin tango. Chloe's skin had to be lime green, she was overflowing with envy.

Without further ado, she pulled Cashay to the corner to get the scoop.

"Uh, huh, what's up with Bionca and Breezy? Don't tell me they fuckin'."

Cashay grinned, "I knew you like my bro's steelo. Look at you getting all jealous. That's B, we talkin' 'bout Chloe. I know you seen her sneaking drinks. She's probably feeling a little nice that's all. Seems like you need a drink to loosen up, too."

Chloe knew better. Bionca may have been tipsy, but she was still throwing herself all over Brezell. Once again, her attempt to get her future man in a civil and reserved way wasn't happening so Chloe added a little mix to the flavor.

She's gotta have it

"John Otis, what's up my guy? The voice said, nervously. Well, umm... I don't mean to call you on no downbeat bullshit, but ya princess is down here at the pool hall showing her ass. She's all over these lil' niggas in here. I mean she is really disrespecting ya name JO."

"I'll be right there!" JO replied, to the disturbing call he received about his diamond. If there was one thing he despised, it was for sure humiliation and disrespect.

When he walked in, it seemed like everybody was concerned except for Chloe. She wasn't even looking up, but the guy whose lap she was sitting in turned his pleasurable smile into a look of alarm. Eventually she noticed and looked back and saw JO approaching with Brezell in tow. She was extremely out of it; maybe it was the ecstasy pill she popped to "loosen up" that had her out of character.

"Hey, daddy. What's up, *Breezy*?" she plainly stated, as cool as a fan, like there wasn't anything wrong with the picture.

JO grabbed her by the arm and pulled her out of the pool hall but not before saying, "Brezell, handle that," and he knew exactly what that meant.

About fifteen minutes later, the party was clearing out and Brezell came back with abraised knuckles. Whatever high Chloe was on automatically went away when she felt the tension and saw the look in her father's shame-filled eyes. She had to know how much of a disgrace she was at that very moment. He looked at her with such disappointment and embarrassment. Chloe sat in silence; out of fear and mostly shame, she was voiceless. If looks could kill, she could've been declared a murder victim. She tried to make an apology to her father to take the chill off.

"Daddy, I'm sorry, I..."

JO instantly cut her off, "Get out of my face, acting like a straight up ho!" He never talked to his princess like that before.

Brezell had never seen him that upset either when they finally made it back to their house.

"Take yo' ass upstairs in ya room and don't come the fuck out unless I tell you to!"

Kim knew better than to say anything that opposed her husband so she settled right back in her bed as quick as she came out of it to see what was going on leaving JO and Brezell a chance to talk.

"Breezy, I don't know what I'm going to do with Chloe, she's growing up so fast," he griped. "Oh and, thanks for handling that lil' nigga for me, he really thought he was doing something slick," he followed referring to the boy Brezell put the beat down on, at the party and slid him $500 for his deed.

"Don't worry about it that man, we fam, and these lil' niggas was trying to earn bragging rights off of shorty, I know the deal." Brezell shook his head in disbelief.

"You's a real lil' dude, you know that? I really don't think Chloe understands her position and status being my daughter. She can't be doing just anything out here and its okay. She's not the same as everybody else."

Brezell sat, caught in his own vile thoughts.

"You okay, Breezy?"

"Awe yeah man, I was thinking 'bout that shit." In reality, he was saying to himself, *what the fuck are you talking about JO? You know Chloe know that shit, but it don't mean a damn thing. She's been try'na give me the pussy for years now. Wake the fuck up! That's why I hate this old ass has-been with a passion.* Out of all the lil' soldiers in his army JO had no idea that Brezell felt this way about him. "JO, you mind if I go talk to her? Maybe she'll understand better if I told her from a younger point of view. Cashay is the same way with my Pops. She doesn't understand."

"Yeah Breezy, that would be cool 'cause I know right now I'm the last person she wants to talk to." He stopped him before Brezell walked off, "Here as a matter of fact, if you don't mind, take her to the mall. That always makes her mom feel better after a fight and she is for sure her mother's child." He counted off more money and gave it to him for Chloe's expenses. "Thanks man and tell her daddy loves her no matter what."

"Alright," Brezell replied as he headed towards Chloe's room.

Chloe's head was buried in a pillow when he entered. She assumed it was her father; automatically she began to apologize.

"Daddy, I'm sorry for shaming your name. I am as embarrassed as you are, but please allow me this time alone right now."

Brezell burst out in laughter, "Enough of that bullshit. Get ya'self together, the King has asked me to take his princess to the mall."

Chloe peeked from under the pillow and saw all 32 of his pearly whites. She was self-conscious and couldn't do anything but laugh at him, blushing and crying at the same time.

"C'mon Baguette, don't cry. You're too pretty for all that and you look a mess when you frown." He made an ugly sad face to cause her to smile again. "On the real though, you were on some bogus shit at that pool hall, what's up with that? I thought you only wanted to show that thing off to me?" All along he wanted her, but she needed to mature a little before he put her down.

She put her head down in degradation blushing again, "I don't know what I was thinking. To tell you the truth, I don't have an explanation," she confessed.

Brezell was so quiet that she had to look up just to see if he had left the room. He sat with a puzzled look on his face.

"Damn, I never realized how much you and Cashay look alike," Brezell remarked staring into her face.

"I know that's why they used to call us twins at school," she said, gleaming back with a smile. Brezell could tell she was thrilled to finally have his undivided attention. "Did daddy really say take me to the mall?" she questioned, ready to roll.

"Yeah, you ready to go?"

"Of course. Daddy may have a Ph.D. in *streetology*, but I sho' in the hell got a master's in *shopology*. Give me a minute to change and I'll ready."

Before long they were en route to the mall.

Once in Brezell's car, he could tell she had fully fallen in love with him posted up in the front seat staring at him at every stop light. Every time he looked over at her, she would blush. Brezell reached over her waist to grab the seat belt just to make her hormones race. He inhaled her scent and memorized it and it was then he became confident he would own her sooner than he thought.

"We follow all safety procedures around this camp," Brezell said, winking his eye. He knew exactly how to get a bitch's panties wet without even touching them.

Inside the mall, he could tell she was anxious to be seen with him. From the outside looking in, it appeared like she was his girl and he was taking her shopping. Whenever she tried things on, she was sure to get his opinion on if it was hot or not.

"Baguette, you know you're a fashion connoisseur. What do you need my approval for?"

"'Cause I do. It matters to me what you think of me."

Brezell thought she just loved the attention. "Whatever, you know you straight. You're a beautiful young lady."

"For real? I thought you never noticed me." She ran from in front of the fitting room three-fold mirrors and gave him a hug.

"Easy," he backed away, "Get ya shop on. JO would kill me if he found out you were all over me."

"I know so, let me do what I do – shop!" Her mood had surely lightening up. She didn't show the wad her father gave her any mercy. She was tearing the walls down at the mall. She purchased a Ferragamo handbag, some Via Spiga sandals, a pair of D&G shades, and a Missoni halter dress.

Brezell, on the other hand, was taking it easy, letting her get her shine on. He bought a pair of Gucci tennis shoes, a Lacosta hat, and a couple of Lacosta polo shirts.

Just about the time when the mall was closing, they bumped into this hoodrat, Brezell had bust down a few times before. He should've known the punk ho would cause a scene; it was in her blood. She called to him from behind and when he seen who it was, he mumbled, "shit!" under his breath. He immediately instructed Chloe, "Go along with the script." Of course she was all game.

"What's up, Breezy, why haven't I heard from you?" the slum ass bitch asked with a frown.

"Awe, what's up Sheila? This is my people Chloe," he replied, with a smirk. "She's the new wifey."

Right on cue, Chloe turned her nose up in the air and replied, "Hey, how you?"

Sheila bucked her eyes, taken aback. "Oh this ya people, huh? Okay, I see how you doing it, it's all gravy baby. How you doing sweetheart? Ya boy tell you how he be raw dogging this good pussy er' whop?"

That statement caught them both off guard.

Without hesitantion Chloe replied, "Naw, but he told me how you can suck a good dick before my time."

Brezell couldn't help but laugh.

Sheila flinched as if she was about to hit Chloe for her slick ass comment, but Brezell wasn't having that. He shot Shelia a demonic stare.

"Ho, you better bounce 'cause where you clown is where you'll get laid the fuck down," he said clinching his jaw.

Sheila looked astonished and rushed off screaming out, "I got you nigga. I'mma make sure child support bank your dog ass."

Brezell threw his arm around Chloe and smiled, "Suck my dick, huh? What you know about that Baguette and you still a virgin?"

"I know a lot, you willing to find out?"

They both snickered at her wit.

It was working; Brezell had her feeling like wifey already. Soon enough it would be reality. Chloe was so busy lusting after him that she totally dismissed Shelia's comment about child support.

Before arriving back to the house, Brezell stopped at TAWK Bookstore. He stared blankly into Chloe's face, wondering why she had a dumbfounded expression about their destination. She followed close behind him as he headed straight to the language department and grabbed a Spanish workbook with a cassette. He also copped a few urban novels. Among those chosen were, Mistress Me, by a newcomer, Venesha, and *In my Peace I trust* by Brittany Davis. He stood pre-occupied reading an article on a new publishing company, Polka Dots and Stripes, then asked, "You want something?" to Chloe.

"Umm, do they sell Bazaar or Style magazines?"

Diary of a Kingpin's Daughter

"Damn, do you ever think about anything else besides material shit? All you think about is clothes, shoes, and fast ways to spend money. You act like those little rich bitches off of that dumb ass movie *Clueless*."

"Whoa, that was way harsh," she replied laughing. Brezell didn't think it was funny how she was quoting a line off of the '90's chic flick he was referring to. He couldn't stand a shallow ass bitch.

"Being JO's daughter is not going to work for you all your life; you better start doing something more constructive and with more substance instead of fucking with those bums," he grilled giving her that evil glare.

Instantly he could tell she was offended by his comments. Her eyes lowered and she bowed her head, once again humiliated. Brezell took a mental note to himself that he would have to toughen her up, make her skin a little thicker than it was.

At the register, he grabbed a Cosmo and a diary from under the counter, ready to check out. He figured he'd give the girlie items to her before she got out the car and he also felt bad for crushing her like that so he tried to initiate small talk to smooth over the small dispute.

"My mom used to keep a diary to release stress." He volunteered the information in the air of the silent car.

Chloe was trying to act all stubborn and shit so fuck, he turned the stereo up and they rode back to the sound of Jay Z through their backs. Twenty minutes later, they arrived to the house; he turned the music down and reached for her hand.

"Look Baguette, I didn't mean to talk to you like that alright."

Chloe did a double take and in Brezell's mind, he knew exactly how to get straight to her heart because he was speaking as if he was JO purposely using the same language as he heard her father using.

With much attitude she replied, "Whatever! Oh and FYI, **BREEZY**, she said with emphasis, I don't fuck and if I did, it wouldn't be with an Indian, it would with the chief. I never really have been into the help!"

Brezell knew he had struck a nerve, Chloe was so angry as soon as they hit the drive way, she already had the door open before he could come to a complete stop.

"Hey," Brezell stopped her before she shut his door. He thought it was so sexy how she turned back towards him in a stank-ass stance. "Here, this is yours." He handed her the bag with the Cosmo magazine and the diary.

"You left something in the bag." She pulled the diary out and tried to hand it back to him.

"Naw, that's for you, it seems like you would like something so girly since it has shoes and purses decorating it. Besides, this is your start to doing something constructive."

Before she could reply, he grabbed the back of her neck to pull her closer to him and gently kissed her pouted lips. It was all tongue action and she was participating fully with every thrust. When Brezell finally stopped, he wanted her to feel light on her feet.

"Grab your other bags out the trunk and call me tomorrow," he demanded instead of asking. Chicks loved that controlling shit. Chloe was no different. She shook her head yes and floated into the house.

Diary of a Kingpin's Daughter

Dear Diary,

I can't believe I'm doing this. This is some real TV type shit. Writing in a diary. And on TV, this is usually how they start off, "Dear diary." That's hilarious, but N-E way, Brezell bought this for me so I'm wit it. I'm glad he did cause now I can spill the beans and not have to worry about it getting out 'cause you won't share my secrets. Brezell mentioned something about his mother keeping a diary and he thought that was cute and very informal after she died. Now that I think about it, I've always wanted a diary; I just never got around to getting one. I love that man. Okay maybe I just like him a lot, but I want to love that man. I want him to break my virginity. He kissed me and it shot fire through my soul. My whole body got warm. I wonder if that's what it feels like when you're in love. He told me to call him tomorrow; I wish he had said call when I get in the house. I'm sho' gone call. How did he know if I had his number? I guess he figure it could be easily accessible.

Brezell –N- Chloe.... Sounds good to me. I can't wait...

It's ya girl,
Chloe Baguette Carter

Real Talk

After the kiss, Brezell and Chloe talked on the phone every day. She never told anyone about the kiss, but the affection she had for him was starting to show. With Cashay gone off to college, even though Chloe had her driving permit and could get a car whenever she wanted, she didn't press the issue because Brezell picked her up everyday after school.

One day, Squeak and Chloe were chilling in Chloe's room and out the blue Squeak asked, "What was up with you and Breezy?"

"What do you mean?" Chloe said, acting dumb.

"Girl, you and Brezell seem to be an item, what's up with that?"

"He's like family, no big deal," she lied.

"Hell naw, I see the way your face lights up whenever he's around and vice versa," she teased. Y'all not fooling anybody, but yourselves."

"I will admit to you that I like him. I like him a lot, but I'm just following his lead." Chloe finally admitted.

"Girl, all I can say is be careful. When you get involved with a man like that, you have to be sure you can handle what comes along with him. And, what the fuck is John Otis gonna say? You must be outta ya mothafuckin' mind." Squeak gave her opinion and gave Chloe a comforting hug. "JO is gonna kill y'all."

The two of them left the conversation alone.

Squeak's outlook made Chloe's mind race; her head overflowed with questions and she knew just the person that may be able to answer them. What better person to ask than one that's been there and done that with a man tough in the game of hustling. Chloe headed straight to her mother's room.

"Mommy, can I talk to you about something?" she whimpered like a baby.

"Of course, baby," Kim replied, while brushing her hair.

"This is some us talk, so please don't tell daddy, okay?"

Kim's eyes widened as she sat down her brush on the vanity. "Oh God, you're pregnant!" she shouted.

"Ma, are you crazy? I'm still a virgin."

"Thank God and on that note, let me know when you're ready for birth control," Kim insisted.

"Mommieee," she huffed. "Anyway, I like this boy. He's a good dude, but he's in the streets and..."

Kim stopped her in mid-sentence, "Baby, I'mma tell you like this, ain't no future in a street nigga. Its short lived. They don't make 'em like John Otis anymore. Niggas ain't wife'n females no more, they using them for all that they can and leaving they asses high and dry. Women are going to jail behind men, nowadays. I remember it was a time when a female didn't do a day because her man took the case. Uh, huh, that shit ain't happenin' in this day and time. Niggas is bitches too, beware! Then if you do luck up on a rare man like your father, life still becomes more difficult. Sometimes I feel like I'm the luckiest women alive, but at times, I also feel like I'm the unfortunate one. Growing up I didn't have good parents to make things happen for me and take care of me, so when I met JO, he was my savior. I vowed that my child would not have to accept the things that I did. I felt as if I didn't have any other choice because without your father, I was nothing. At least that's what I thought. Don't get me wrong, princess, I love you more than I love my next breath, but like I said, the streets don't love anybody." Kim's eyes watered as she continued.

Chloe felt so bad for making her express those unwanted emotions, although she wanted her to continue giving her the game.

"When you deal with a man of the street, there are as many bad days as there are good. For instance, I've stayed up many nights worried to death, wondering if my husband would be come home or not. I'd pray he hadn't been busted by the police or killed. Then there are all the other females. I used to prepare myself for those, 'I'm pregnant by John Otis' calls. Baby, its so much drama and stress attached to being a hustler's wife. Before your dad was as big as he is now, we had to be accompanied by others when we went places, in fear someone would kidnap us for ransom or rob me because of who your father was. That changed somewhat over time when your dad let it be known, he ain't no fuck type nigga. But still, in all, who wants to live like that? Baby, I can't change your heart, all I can say is nothing in this world is worth your life. You are so precious and you deserve nothing but the best. I can't tell you not to fool with the young man because he's in the streets because that would be condescending and I'd be forcing you to sneak, but at least let your daddy know you're trying to fuck Brezell before the streets tell him."

That caught Chloe by total surprise. She didn't bother to ask her mom how she knew the facts. The obvious was observable.

Diary of a Kingpin's Daughter

Dear Diary,

It's official. I'm a woman...Brezell's woman! Last night we went to a nice intimate dinner at Ruth's Chris' and talked extensively. He surely had his grown man thing going. It's like he knows exactly what to say and how to say it to me. He kept whispering in my ear how he's been waiting forever to love me. Made my panties wet for sure.

"I'm that nigga baby, and you that chic. We gonna make the world jealous, Baguette," he assured me.

When I say my heart was in tune to his every word, please believe it. He gently rubbed the nape of my neck playing with my oversized Shirley Temple curls and I almost melted. I was ready for a doggie bag and anxious for him to do me doggie-style!

After we had dinner and I lied to my mom about me staying over Cashay's, Brezell got a room for us. Well, actually, he already secured the room I just had to secure my lie. The room was decorated especially for me. Rose peddles spread across the bed; rose scented pink candles lit the room and R. Kelly's, Chocolate Factory graced the C.D. player. All of this for the young girl? I was beyond impressed and feeling like I matured two years. I had a thug with a sensitive side and I loved every bit of this scene. When I peeked inside the Jacuzzi, it was milk-bath filled and surrounded by pink rose petals.

Diary of a Kingpin's Daughter

Brezell pulled me down on the bed and kissed me passionately. When he stood up to undress, my heart beat uncontrollably when he removed his boxers. I thought I was going to die! My guy was packin'! Hung low as Cashay would say. I was terrified; I didn't know how that big thing would fit inside of little ole' virgin me. And, I know he knew what I was thinking because his ass had that cocky-ass smirk on his face as it dangled in front of me. With fear in my eyes and all, Brezell picked me up and carried me over to the Jacuzzi where we enjoyed our first milk bath together. I felt so special. He kissed my neck and ears so tenderly.

"Are you ready to go to ecstasy?" he asked, tongue kissing my ears.

Without hesitation, he slid down under my wobbly legs and instantly took me there. Kissing, licking and sucking my pearl tongue like he had struck gold. OMG! This was the best feeling I'd ever had in my life! My legs continued to tremble. I didn't know if I should stop him before I fainted from pleasure or hold his ass down so he couldn't get up!!

He carried me back to the bed and dried off my dripping body, mostly with his tongue and some with a towel. When he laid me down, a tear rolled from both eyes. I was so fuckin' scared of penetration.

"I'll take is slow, but it will hurt briefly."

He held me for a minute and swirled it around my tightness until he could ease it in. I still couldn't believe I was giving it all to him and the shit hurt like hell! Pain is pleasure so I held it down, but it didn't stop me from fuck faces.

All I know is after that, he was mine and I was his! I already loved this man.

Chloe –n-Brezell 4ever!
It's ya gurl,
Chloe Baguette Carter

The beginning of a beautiful union...

Finally, after months and months of talking on the phone and indirect courting, Brezell finally asked Chloe to be his girl. He was four years older than she was and much more advanced. She gave him her adolescence and allowed him to turn her into a woman. Their secret was out; everybody knew they were an item. As opposed to what they thought, John Otis wasn't upset at all. In fact, he was pleased to have Brezell play his part. He was mostly content that he was somebody he knew personally and could keep a close eye on. This also helped Brezell come up more – money and status wise – him being JO's daughter's boyfriend alone upgraded him. Brezell was making more moves, which meant making more dough.

The two had become inseparable. They became best friends, sharing deep intimate feelings and Brezell was right, they made a lot of people jealous. The hotel stays increased and so did the love making.

Most of Chloe's friends were happy that she finally snagged him. Everybody was interested in the Brezell stories. At first, Bionca seemed a bit jealous. Chloe even mentioned It to Brezell, but he brushed it off.

"Don't no dame like being on the outside looking in and she think she's the prettiest bitch anyway? Get the fuck outta here! She probably thought a nigga wanted her ass," he drew to conclusion.

This made Chloe think back to the pool party when Bionca was all in Brezell's grill. He told her not to worry about it and she didn't because when he said not to worry about something, it was no need to second-guess a real dude.

One night, Brezell and Chloe went down to Navy Pier, an arcade and restaurant built on to Lake Michigan, as part of downtown Chicago. There, he confided his deepest secrets to her.

"Don't think I'm crazy for telling you this, but I don't think Monty is my real father."

"What! What would make you think he's not?"

The cool water rocked back and forth as both of them stared out ocean.

"I found my mother's diary and read it. At first, I didn't want to read it, but in a way I did, to find out why she did this to herself. So, as I'm reading, I learned that she was cheating on Monty."

"OMG!"

This confused the hell out of Chloe because in her opinion, Brezell looked just like

Money Green. Brezell was hurt when he went into further detail about his mother's adultery.

"Do you know how that shit makes me feel? Fucked up, that's how! I want to go to Monty about it, but if I do, and we find out he's not my father, I'm fucked."

"Umm, it'll be okay," she uncertainly replied, trying to comfort her man.

"No, it won't. You don't understand because you're not in my position. It's a nigga out there right now saying to himself, 'I could be that lil' nigga's daddy.' And that's a fucked up feeling."

Chloe was lost for words.

"I'm thinking Monty's not my real father anyway. He's a weak ass man. JO's flunky. Man, I've been lost respect for him." Sounds of hostility graced his vocals. He squeezed his eyes tight when he told this part of his history, like he was looking at it happen again. "I can remember it like it was yesterday," he stated in a mild angry tone. "I come rolling down Wentworth Ave. on one of the hottest days of the summer, on a mountain bike, and I see Monte's sorry ass standing above JO with a damn umbrella, blocking the sun for this grown ass man, like a servant, just like a dam send off dude! At that very minute, I knew I didn't want to be nothing like his do-boy ass when I got older. He would never be considered my hero. The only thing that I did respect him for was loving my mother unconditionally and taking care of her through her Bipolar condition. I guess him taking care of Cashay and me, too. I can give him that much. Shit, coming up though, I wanted to be like John Otis not like no mothafuckin' Money Green."

Brezell shook his head in disgust. He had this stone cold look on his face; his whole demeanor changed like he was sitting there looking at Monte holding the umbrella, all over again. Chloe didn't say anything mostly because she was scared that she would say the wrong thing. She couldn't do anything other than offer him her gentle touch so, she rubbed his back, held him close, and told him it was going be okay.

"Baby, I'm always here for you. Fuck everybody else. It's you and me 'til the end."

"Man, I never thought I'd be able to love a woman until the day I fell in love with you. You mine forever, Baguette."

The feelings he claimed to have for Chloe were all-new emotions for him; he said that she made him feel complete. That night they talked for hours about any and everything. If there was anything Chloe wanted him to say to her, it seemed like he said it all in one night.

Two weeks later, Brezell got Baguette tattooed on his forearm designed around a huge diamond. Under it read, "Next best thing to a soldier" and Chloe had Jonathan, Brezell's real name tatted inside of a tiny heart on her lower abdomen.

Dear Diary,

I never knew love could be like this. Brezell is all I can think about these days. How can one person have such an effect on my heart? I love this man with every fiber in my body, with every breath I take. I feel so close to him. We tell each other everything; at this point I can't imagine my world without him. I wish it was something I could do to heal his pain, when he hurts, I hurt. I'm glad he was my first, and I can tell he will be my only. I never thought I could have so much love for another man like I love my father, with such strong emotion. Truth be told Brezell is in a very high standing and I hope this feeling never goes away. If it's left up to me, we will be together forever and a day. This I know for sure.
Brezell is my Breezy!

It's ya gurl
Chloe Baguette Carter

I'ma Grown Ass Woman
3 years later...

At 18, Chloe was doing what some women awaited a lifetime for. She was in her last year of high school living it up like a made man's woman. For their 3-year anniversary, Brezell and Chloe flew to New York for a shopping spree and from New York to Cancun for 3 nights. JO had taken Chloe all over the world, but for some reason, she felt like she'd never been out of Chicago while traveling with her man. She had no idea Brezell was so tasteful. He really stepped his game up since the two of them hooked up. He was driving the finest cars, wearing the trendiest gear, and making presidential moves. Brezell mentioned he had something important to talk to her about, but didn't want to talk in the rental car or the hotel. Chloe anxiously waited three days through Cancun until they arrived back in New York before he laid it on her thick.

"You love me, right?" Brezell asked, in his raspy voice.

"Yeah, you know I do," she replied, with a curious look on her face. Chloe knew that when he started off his sentence with 'you love me, right,' he wanted something from her.

"Well, I need you to show me now, more than ever, and you're the only one I can trust."

"Bay, you know I'm down for my nigga, its whatever." Chloe chose her words too soon because no sooner than she let "whatever" slide off her tongue, he was asking her to throw bricks at a women's federal correctional institute.

"I want you to let me tape this work to you when we get ready to fly back home." Chloe widened her eyes as she dug in her ears. She thought maybe she heard him wrong.

"What? Are you crazy?" Chloe didn't think she could bring herself to do it. She would die if she got caught or JO would kill them both if he got wind of it. "Does JO know?" she questioned.

Brezell quickly grew angry, "Fuck no and you better not tell him, I'm trying to make my own moves. I'm not about to keep being spoon fed by your muthfuckin' daddy. Can't a nigga branch off? Can't a nigga provide for his future wife without her daddy?"

Chloe stared at him teary eyed as the steam ran threw her nose and turned into snot, afraid to say no and much more, afraid to say yes.

"Baby, I love you, and I would never let anything happen to you. If I didn't think it would be okay, I wouldn't even ask you to do this."

In between sniffs, she asked, "Well if it's okay, than why can't you tape it to you?"

He was starting to become irritated, "You said you loved me, you said you were down for whatever, now you're questioning me.. I made a promise to always take care of you." His tone of voice began to terrify her.

Chloe became baffled and lost for words.

Brezell read her body language and softened his voice to get what he wanted. "Chloe Baguette, you are my diamond, you are my world. I would never put your life in danger or do anything to hurt you. I could have easily got one of the rats out the hood, they would have done it for an outfit, pair of stilettos, topped by a good fuck, but I didn't cause, baby, we don't hold any secrets from each other. You're my Bonnie and I'm your Clyde. Baby, this is a power move for us. With this connect, the streets are ours."

By now, her tears were streaming. "But what about JO?"

Fury visited his voice again, but this time his eyes had a cold stare. "I'm not Monte, I'm not about to live in yo daddy's shadow for the rest of my life. I'm my own man and I wanna make my own moves. I mean we fam and all, no love lost, but I wanna eat off my own plate."

That statement made her very upset. To Chloe, it sounded like he was trying to knock her father out the box and take over, like those two white mice, Pinky and The Brain who always had an idea to take over and rule the world.

"So you're saying fuck my daddy?"

Brezell knew that man was her soft spot so he rephrased his comment and tried choosing his words more carefully in fear of running her off and telling his plan.

"Baby girl, soon you will be Mrs. Jonathan Wright. We don't want to have to live off of your father for the rest of our lives. What happens when he's not here? Don't you want your man, your husband, to be able to hold you down on his own?"

Brezell had a point, but she also didn't want the two men she loved most to cross each other. Chloe wanted so badly to be his wife and even she knew JO wouldn't be there for them forever so what he didn't know wouldn't hurt.

With that in mind, she allowed Brezell to tape the two bricks to her body under a girdle, and they flew back to Chicago.

Diary of a Kingpin's Daughter

Dear Diary,

Everything is moving so fast for me right now. I have a few months left of high school and daddy is pressuring me to go out of state for school, but Brezell is begging me to stay. Sometimes I feel like I'm being pulled between the two men I love the most. I notice that Brezell always wants me to do the opposite of everything daddy wants. Not just the college thing, but everything. It's like he intentionally has the opposite answer as daddy. I'm constantly torn between the two men in my life.

Brezell asked me to move in with him. I haven't mentioned it to daddy yet, but I already know he won't approve of it. He already complained about me never being home. Daddy asked me what Brezell's been up to. I guess everybody is starting to notice him having major paper. Daddy knows all the moves his soldiers make and he thinks its mighty funny Brezell seems to be holding down more money than accounted for. I just told daddy that Brezell has been saving and now he's starting to splurge. I know daddy is nobody's fool, I just hope he don't find out about Brezell's connect in New York.

Yeah and, somebody has been playing on my phone. Calling, making fucking noises, and saying Brezell's name. I haven't brought it to him yet, 'cause I know how ho's hate, and I don't want to sound petty, but let me find out that nigga fucking off on me.

It's ya girl,
Chloe Baguette Carter

Will you?

High school graduation, a day that seemed to take forever to come for Chloe finally arrived. In tradition of their partying family, Chloe and Squeak were thrown a big celebration. Squeak enlisted in the Army and even though no one could figure why, they commemorated her joining. Chloe had applied and gotten accepted to Prairie State Community College to begin classes to become a Dental Technician. She thought by staying in state for college, it would please both of the men in her life. And, it worked.

Everybody who was somebody was at the extravaganza JO threw for the girls at a well known local club that he frequented. All of the girls from *The Untouchables* finally had a chance to reunite for the first time in a year. Especially since Taylor and Cashay were still residing in Houston, TX for college and seldom came home. Bionca and Chloe kept in touch, but were not as close since the crew went separate ways. Chloe thought this day was one of the most memorable days of her life; besides the day she became Brezell's wifey.

Chloe hadn't seen Brezell since they entered the club together and she found that odd especially since, he loved for her to only be a step or two away from his view. Using this free time to mingle, Chloe walked through the crowd, but her rhythm was broken by congratulators pinning bills on her shirt. Although, she was thankful, she wanted to find JO to see what gift he had in store for her. She walked past the back of the club to the bathroom attempting to open it. As she began to open it, Bionca came stumbling out holding her stomach. Bionca didn't even look at up at Chloe nor, did she acknowledge her. When Chloe called out to her, Bionca kept it moving. Chloe peeked inside the bathroom and it smelled terrible; B had vomited all over the floor.

Back mingling with the crowd, Chloe chatted it up with her girls.

"Cashay, what's it like in H-Town? What's it hittin' for?" Chloe knew Cashay would have the scoop.

"Uh, uh, my question is who hit up Bionca? You know that bitch is pregnant."

"What?" Taylor, Squeak, and Chloe sang.

"C'mon, stop playin'. Y'all knew that. Chloe you need to talk to ya girl since you the only one staying here. You definitely gonna need to be the T-T to her baby and hold it down for those of us away."

"Fa sure," Chloe promised. "Anyway, where did she go?"

"Girl, she left talking about she needs to rest." Cashay informed them. "I told her, we'd get up with her tomorrow or sometime before we leave."

The girls were in the middle of the floor clowning with Kim and Aunt Ryan when out of nowhere Brezell got on the mic.

"Excuse me," echoed loudly through the building gaining him everyone's attention. The DJ lowered *Dangerously in Love* by Beyoncé to a whisper in the background. "Can I have everyone's attention, especially Chloe's please?"

He caught her glance and flashed his signature smile, which made her blush with a grin from ear-to-ear. She had no idea what Brezell was up to, but whatever it was, JO was in on it as well. It was most obvious that is was something important since he stood beside Brezell in support.

"Chloe Baguette Carter, with the permission from your father, John Otis Carter, I ask you to be my wife, Mrs. Jonathan Wright."

The whole room in unity bellowed, "*AWWWW*," applauding at the same time. Chloe was in total shock. Kim grabbed and hugged her as they both rejoiced. Brezell stood frozen with a blue box in his hand. It was highly noticeable that it was the signature color of Tiffany & Company. She floated towards the stage where he waited nervously for her response.

"Will you?" He asked again with a nervous grin.

"Of course. I mean, yes, I'd love to be your wife," she managed to get out with a cracking voice.

Brezell pulled out a 4-carat platinum diamond ring. A perfect fit for her size 5 finger. JO hugged her tightly and a second after grabbed the microphone from Brezell.

"Breezy." JO got real serious, "this woman is **my** Baguette, she means the world to me and I trust you with her life. So, everybody witnessing, this man gave me his word. If anything happens to my baby, nigga you owe me your life! Welcome to my family, mothafucka. When's the date?"

Brezell grabbed the mic back without fear, "Sometime in July, nigga," he teased him back.

Since the two already had a sit down, Brezell knew the rules. JO even helped him pick out Chloe's ring.

Damn, my baby just signed his life over to daddy. He must love me! She mused to herself.

A week after the party, Brezell added another tat to his body. This time he got Chloe trimmed in blood on his neck.

Diary of a Kingpin's Daughter

Dear Diary,

I's a woman now! Lol! I can't believe I'm out of the nest already, I never thought I would go straight from my parent's house to the big leagues. It's all good though cause my baby can hold it down, not quite like daddy, but my boo got me! I'm so excited. I worked it out so that I could please both daddy and Brezell. I'm going to school so that pleases daddy, and it's within city limits so you know Brezell was satisfied. My graduation party was the shit! It was like a coming out party for me. I am so happy and so blessed. I'm floating and nothing can take this feeling away. I can't wait to start decorating our spot! I can't stop smiling. I just wanna scream to myself, "This is it Chloe! This is it! All that I've been waiting for and all that I've wanted! Just my Breezy and me! It's on! It's on and it's on!"

It's ya girl,

Chloe Baguette Carter soon to be Carter-Wright

To be or not to be...

Without question, Chloe moved out of her parent's 5-bedroom mini mansion and into a 3-bedroom loft with her new fiancé. She was due to begin college the following fall. Life was indeed good and she didn't have any complaints. She managed to make both the men in her life happy hoping they would become one big blissful family. Every Sunday, they either ate with JO and Kim or they went out to dinner.

One particular night, Kim suggested that Chloe help her prepare dinner. She wanted to talk to her daughter about some things. Chloe could tell by the tone that her mother wanted to have another serious talk.

"Mom, how do you make chicken and dumplings?" she asked, while stirring the cornbread mix.

"Whoa baby, you moving too fast." Kim laughed at Chloe's eagerness. "Baby, you got to learn how to make chicken first. At this point, you would burn water!"

Both of them shared a laugh.

"Now, let's get to the real talk. Baby, how does it feel to be engaged and have a live-in man?"

Chloe thought carefully before answering, "So far so good. I can't complain. Naw, I take that back, I have one complaint. I hate when he comes in at all times of the night. I always compare us to you and daddy. Daddy always came in at 12 am, regardless of what was going on."

Kim smirked before she spoke. "How do you know? You were always in the bed and supposed to be sleep. Although, you're right, he did," she laughed.

"I might have been in the bed, but I didn't fall asleep until I heard my daddy come home. I started doing that at 7-years-old, until the day I moved out."

Kim laughed, "You know you're a daddy's girl if I've ever met one." Her expression became serious with her next statement. "Baby girl, you're not just marrying that man, you're marrying the game. You realize this, don't you?"

With that last remark, John Otis walked in the kitchen, first kissing Kim and then, Chloe on the forehead.

"What are my two favorite women in her gossiping about?" He asked leaning against the refrigerator. "Naw, I don't want to hear that, but I do want to hear how my baby doing out on her own. That nigga taking good care of you? Don't even answer that 'cause if he ain't, I'll buss that lil' nigga. Anyway, how's school?"

Chloe gleamed like a little girl, while holding her dad's hand like she used to do when she was a kid.

"Its good daddy, but I think I want to change my major to journalism, but other than that college is cool."

JO had a puzzled look on his face.

"How in the hell you go from a Dental Tech to a Journalist?"

"Because I really want to be a writer."

Before the conversation could continue, Brezell walked in with his million-dollar smile. She dazed at her soon-to-be husband in admiration.

Oh wee, my baby is fine! My baby stuntin' like my daddy.

Brezell interrupted her mirror image thinking. "I know y'all not holding a town meeting without me."

Brezell and JO grabbed each other by the hands and did a manly embrace. Followed by a kiss on Kim's cheek, and turned to Chloe and kissed her forehead, as JO had just done moments before. JO slightly smirked, knowing Brezell tried hard to play him.

"Dag ma, what's for dinner? It smells good!" Brezell said peeking in the pot as Kim smacked his hand playfully. It was all love.

John Otis was in high spirits and so was Brezell, which meant everything to Chloe, and made her glow with happiness.

At dinner, JO kept staring at them as his Baguette fed Brezell and wiped his mouth when she missed her target. Brezell knew deep down JO hated seeing that he turned his daughter into a woman. After a few seconds of watching them, he turned to his wife and started a one-on-one conversation, although he talked loud enough for everyone to hear.

"Ya know baby, if I didn't know any better, I would say the two of them, are us, damn near 20 years back, so youthful, and genuinely in love just like we were and still are." JO smiled at Brezell and commented, "Breezy, I wish your momma was here to see this, she's probably smiling in her grave. I'm sure she never seen this one coming. You two despised each other when you were kids."

Brezell clinched his jaw and grew tense when John Otis made that comment, trying to keep his composure. His only response was, "Ummp," real fake like. He tried to cover it up, hoping his girl didn't notice it.

"For real, daddy? I can barely remember that!" she said trying to imagine it.

"You probably wouldn't 'cause y'all was too young, still had breast milk in ya mouth." He chuckled his old wise man cackle that Brezell hated so much. "On the real though, neither one of you probably remember 'cause you were so small and by the time y'all probably grew a good memory, hell, y'all was doing y'all own things by then."

Brezell let out a phony laugh all the while thinking, *No this bitch ass nigga didn't speak of my moms like he really gave a fuck about her. I shoulda told his ho ass to watch his mouth, it's his fault she's no longer alive.*

Before they left, Kim made plans to meet Chloe at the spa to continue their girl talk. Purposely, Brezell was quiet and irritable the entire ride home.

When they arrived home, he immediately got in the shower, got dressed and left without saying a word to Chloe. She tried calling his cell phone, but he allowed the phone to ring what seemed like 20 times before he answered it. When he finally answered, Chloe sat silent, listening to his back ground. As he started to speak, a small child in the background, learning how to talk, called out, "Da-dee, phone, phone, hello," cheerfully.

Damn! Brezell thought, not in the mood for explaining.

The first thing Chloe asked was, "Where are you and who baby is that?"

Brezell huffed loud enough so that she could hear his frustration.

"Man, I'm getting tired of you always calling, questioning me and shit. I'm at my guy house! That's his shawty talking and I guess you need to know, who is my guy too, right? Listen, just because we're engaged It doesn't mean you have the right to ask a nigga a boatload of questions."

Then came another loud huff, but this time it came from outside the phone and it was Brezell's mistress's irritation. He didn't really know how much longer he would be able to keep her hyper ass under the radar.

Chloe began to snap, "I guess that's your guy's girl too, huh?" she screamed, disbelieving his defense.

"Stop asking so many fucking questions, what are you, the police now? You need to ask your damn father why the hell he gotta talk about my muthafuckin mom, that's what the fuck you need to be asking!" Brezell hung up on her and didn't return home for the rest of the night.

After getting what seemed like the best head in the world, he was forced to fall asleep to his comforter's heartbeat.

Diary of a Kingpin's Daughter

Dear Diary,

For the first time since we moved in together, Brezell did not come home. The feelings and thoughts I had running through my head were like torture. I kept imaging him with another girl, talking to her, holding her, and smiling at her like he does me. My stomach couldn't take that, it kept turning and a balling up like the feeling you get when you're nervous or anxious. I guess he had an attitude 'cause my daddy mentioned his mom. I knew that was his soft spot, but I didn't know speaking of her was forbidden. Personally, I think he overreacted. That probably was just his excuse to spend the night with some bitch. Don't sleep, boo boo, I'm not no dumb broad.

When I heard that baby talking in the background, I felt nauseous. A short-term rumor passed through that Brezell fathered a child. I never found out anything factual, no names, no baby pictures, or real proof, besides hearsay, with nothing to back it up. Yet, I still allowed it to sit in the back of my head on reserve. I'm going to find out who the fuck house he was supposedly over. I know he's lying, wait 'till he walks his ass through the door. He really gonna call me the police 'cause his ass is gonna be under a straight up interrogation around this bi-itch.

Please don't let this man be cheating on me. I don't know if I could handle knowing. Shit, I definitely know I can't handle another bitch giving my man a baby before me. OOOOH! That would be the worst. Hopefully these Tylenol PMs will kick in real soon so I can be forced to rest my mind and sleep.

It's ya girl,

Chloe Baguette Carter

♪It's morning and he slept the night away♪

When Chloe awoke the next morning, Brezell was still not home. She really didn't want anybody to know that she and Breezy weren't the perfect couple they seemed to be. She was hesitant to call venting to anybody, but at the same time, she didn't want to leave the house, fearing he would come while she was out. Then she would miss confronting him or even worse, he wouldn't come home another night.

Chloe swallowed her pride and called Squeak first. She was now living in St. Louis with her lover, Jade, which is also where her Army base was stationed. It was 8:00 in the morning so Chloe figured she should be up, assuming all soldiers got up with the sun, just like in her father's army.

"Hellooo?" a soft, sleepy voice said, sounding annoyed into the phone. A voice that wasn't Squeak's, but one Chloe recognized.

"Hey Jade, I'm sorry, did I wake you?" she asked in an apologetic tone.

"Yeah, but Squeak is up, as usual, with the damn birds. I don't know why her ass did not answer the phone." Before Jade could holler for

Squeak to pick up the phone, Squeak was already commenting on her not rushing to answer it first.

"Cause its time to get yo lazy ass up! Chloe, I got me a lazy ass broad. Hang up the phone and get yo ass up!" Squeak chimed playfully in the phone.

"Whatever, I'm sleepy. Fucking around with you all night, I missed my full 12 hours of sleep. Chloe, don't people pose ta get at least 12 hours of rest each night?" Jade asked in her southern twang.

Squeak answered before Chloe could, "Naw, you lazy cow, it's 6. Now hang up the damn phone telling all our business." She blew kisses into the phone playfully. "I love you too," she said to Squeak. "Take care, Chloe." and she hung up the phone.

Jade was Squeak's live-in lover. Yes, she became a lesbo, a carpet muncher, had her lick-her license for some time now. She came out of the closet after she left for the Army. She said she had always liked girls, but wouldn't dare fuck off like that while she still lived at home so she disguised it with little made-up boyfriends. When the family found out, everybody stop talking to her except for Chloe. She was the only one who didn't judge her and loved her just the same.

Aunt Ryan's heart was broken. "I didn't raise no fucking fag ass carpet munchers! That pussy bumping shit is nasty and I will not claim a daughter that prides the devil like that," she would say referring to Squeak, her only daughter, as if she herself was the Virgin Mary. Ryan needed to stop because it was heard back in her day she was Ms. Experiment Queen, so what did she label herself, bi-curious?

"What's up cuzo, you up early," Squeak said, drinking a bottle of water.

"I know girl, I need to talk, I got bfb," Chloe stated, both of them remembering what having "boyfriend blues" meant from high school, before Squeak's pussy hounding days. Something made a loud thump in Squeak's background startling Chloe on the other end of the phone.

"Damn girl, what was that? It sound like Jade just dropped yo ass for waking her up," Chloe chimed, trying to sound the least bit cheery.

"Gull please, I wear the pants around this piece. I dropped a weight trying to move it with one hand," she said in the southern accent she had become accustomed to. "But what's up with you? I know I don't need to come home and wreck shop on that nigga, do I?"

"Calm down little boy from the hood!" Chloe said, laughing at how thugged out Squeak had become; trying to play her role as the more dominant partner.

"Yeah, laugh when I come whoop yo nigga ass if he not treating my fav person good, shawty. 'Cause my arms 'bout big as ya boi's by now. His ass still skinny as hell?" she asked.

Chloe laughed so hard at the thought of seeing Squeak beat the shit out of Brezell. He would just shoot her if he couldn't win.

"But for real, Chloe, what's up?"

"Alexis Keys, if you repeat this conversation to anybody, I will kill you," she said to Squeak as serious as she knew how. Squeak knew it was serious, especially since Chloe called her by her full name.

"Gull, pah-leeze, I can't help it if you want everybody to think your relationship is like Jada Pinkett-Smith and Will Smith, but any how, who I'm gon tell, my bitch? Shit, she don't care 'bout shit but shopping, eating, sleeping, and letting me play with that...,"

Chloe cut her off before she could finish, "Too much information, hun. I get the picture!" she retorted before Squeak said something that needed a parental advisory sticker or a bleep noise over it.

"Whatever. I'm all ears, boo, so express yourself." Squeak offered a listening ear.

Chloe started off by filling her in on the events surrounding Brezell not coming home. "My dad made mention of Tina. You remember her, Cashay and Brezell's mom. Anyway, he started reminiscing about when we were kids, and Tina used to bring him over our house and that's what seemed to run him off when we got home.

"So what's that got to do with shit?"

"Well, you know how sensitive that issue is; his mother committed suicide."

"Oh yeah, that's right. That's real fucked up."

"So listen Squeak, before that, this shit was already going down. First off, some bitch has been playing on my phone. It started off with her saying Brezell's name and moaning as if they were fucking like she purposely dialed my number and laid the phone down. This has been happening for a while and I refuse to get my number changed for some chickenhead, hoodrat, and sack chasing bum-bitch. Most of the calls come in with a blocked ID, some calls are silent calls, and now most of the time when I pick up, a baby would be repeatedly saying 'Dah-Dah, Dah-dee,' and then the dial tone. I figure the calls mostly come when the trick doesn't know where Brezell is and hasn't seen him so she checks to see if we're together."

"Damn Chloe, sounds like you got a stalker. Have you ever brought the shit to Breezy?" Squeak asked, choking on her water.

"Yep. And once, he just so happened to be right there when I got one of the calls from the baby. I just handed him the phone and said, 'Here, your baby wants to talk to you,' and let him hear, 'Daa-dah, dah-dee'."

"I bet that nigga shitted his pants!" Squeak said, laughing.

"Naw, you would think, but instead he got mad at me and said I'm starting to stay on some dumb shit. He had the nerve to tell me I'm gon get enough of playing detective. Like I called the damn baby. I didn't want him to stay mad at me so I just let it go."

"Naw baby girl, you can't keep letting shit go, that's when a nigga take your kindness for weakness, and then they start running over your ass. Chloe, a nigga only do what you let him, take it from a nigga that know."

They both laughed.

"Girl, I get so much trim around this bitch, I'm starting to feel like a real live man. I see why men flip out over hos. Pussy is good and addicting. I'm a player. A straight pimp. I turn a straight ho crooked with this game!" Squeak said playfully.

"I heard that!!! You better check yo self," Jade shouted in the background.

"Girl, you know I don't want to hear that fag shit," Chloe joked.

They both laughed, sounding just like a comment her Aunt Ryan would make.

"But back to the subject, boo, you should fly down here to STL for a few days and relax. I'll take care of you fa sho, just get here. Jade just asked when you was gon' come through so she can put a face to the voice, besides pictures and shit. She wants to meet her cuz-in-law. You can stay here. Shit, be ghost on that nigga and let him see how it feels."

That was music to Chloe's ears; she felt she needed a trip in her life.

"Okay, cool. What y'all malls looking like?" she asked. Shopping was always better than therapy for Chloe.

"Aww, wench, I knew yo ass was going to make me have to spend some money this weekend cause soon as yo ass get to shopping, Jade gon think she got to too," Squeak said already picturing Jade's hand out. "But on the real, I'll have her take you to the Galleria. I know that's your style. Shit, I stick to Westfield Mall, the hood mall, where you can get tennis shoes, your hair braided, and rims in one stop. It reminds me of Ever Green Plaza in the Chi, you know I keeps it gully," Squeak said, trying to sound masculine.

"Bye girl, let me get some shit together and go get an oil change on the Range and I'm there. Ohh wait, you gon let Jade take me to the club? The co-ed club where guys like girls and visa versa," she hollered before Squeak could answer the first part of the question.

"Fa sho, you know I don't force my lifestyle on nobody. I'll go too; it's always cracking at this club called Sprulls and the Spotlight. Just hit me when you on the E-way. Love you, Chloe."

"I love you too, Squeak." Before Chloe could make a move, her phone rang. "Hello?"

"Don't play no games, baby girl, come for real, its only 3 ½ hours," she expressed.

"I know. I'm there, if you let me get it together."

They immediately began to plan for the weekend.

Before Chloe made any moves, she called her parents to tell them her plans.

"Hey mom, just wanted to let you know me and the girls are traveling to Squeak's this weekend in the Lou for an all girls weekend."

"That sounds nice, but did your man approve of 'all girls' weekend?"

"What kinda question is that? Of course, he's cool with it." She lied, and didn't catch on to what Kim was really trying to say.

"Well, you young ladies have fun but stop and see us before you leave. Hold up, your dad wants to talk to you."

"You wanna explain to me about this 'all girls' weekend with Squeak. You know I heard about her and her live-in female lover."

"Daddy, don't be silly. Squeak ain't trying to turn nobody out, only if they want to," Chloe laughed, knowing how JO felt about "gay-ism," as he referred to it.

"Them damn people disgust me. They got they own shit going on; communities, languages, schools, jobs, all that shit."

John Otis had what they called homophobia and even though Squeak was family, he too shut her out, cut her off just like he would do a complete stranger. Kim was more understanding of the situation, but only dealt with Squeak when she was in her presence. Nobody called her or interacted with her except for Chloe. She didn't care what nobody thought; Squeak was still her cousin and her favorite one at that.

The truth of the matter was Chloe hardly talked to Cashay and Taylor. Ever since they left for college, they had their own lives going on and rarely came home or kept in touch. Like the good saying goes; out of sight, out of mind. Bionca was always preoccupied with caring for her son, so she didn't have much time to hang out. They were always cordial when they did see each other, they always talked in each other's presence like the relationship hadn't changed, but they left it at just that, a cordial conversation. Sometimes Chloe wished she could be more of a "TT" to Bionca's son, Johnson, now one year old.

Chloe was just so caught up in Brezell she didn't have extra energy or time to revive her friendship with the only crew member that still resided in the same city.

Hours had passed and still Brezell did not come home and the power was off on his phone. Chloe started thinking the worst. Maybe he got arrested, maybe he was in the hospital, maybe he was somewhere hurt, and this is not like him; *something has to be wrong*. After calling what seemed like every hospital, jail, and morgue, checking by his name and John Doe, Chloe called the person that would know if he was okay or not. She just wanted to know was the nigga breathing or not. Brezell had already coached her on worst-case scenarios so she knew not to call certain people looking for him or make any conspicuous comments to people. She was kind of hesitant to even call, but was worried so she let go of his hour-by-hour "rule of the game" ethics he felt he was installing in her. First, she called Monte Wright.

"Hey, Money Green, how are you?" Chloe greeted, pretending to be happy and smiling.

"Hey how's my favorite daughter-in-law?"

"Your favorite daughter-in-law? I better be your only daughter-in-law," she half-joked.

"You know what I mean, but how are you anyway?" he asked. Knowing how girls take shit and run with it he tried to clean it up, "I see you got my son over there sprung, girl. I never thought he would settle down like he has. You're working on your foundation over there and I know it will be beautiful when it's complete," he said.

"Yeah, Money Green, we trying. It's not easy, but we doing it. Speaking of your son, I was calling to see if he was over there or had you heard from him?" she asked trying to sound like it wasn't a concern, but more just a question.

"Naw, he not here. I haven't seen him since last night when he came and got two to-go plates for you guys to eat. Komara, my lady friend, hooked up two plates for y'all. Is something wrong?" he asked, not knowing he really just did more than open up a can of worms. He dropped the damn can and it wasn't a can of worms, it was snakes.

That bastard not just lying up with a ho, he feeding the bitch too! Oh hell to the naw, she thought to herself. She tried to play it off, not trying to give away how his statement had surprised her.

"Oh, that's who cooked that food? I knew it was too seasoned to be from a restaurant," she said hoping to sound convincing.

"So you liked the spaghetti and all?"

"Fa sho," she said hoping he didn't ask how the meat tasted.

"Well, I'm glad you liked it. I'll tell Komara that was a thank you. What do you want me to tell Brezell if I see him?" he asked ending their conversation as Komara walked in the room.

"Aww, it's nothing, I was just gon' tell him he left his cell phone and remind him to stop at the cleaners. Don't worry about it Money, you don't even have to tell him I called," she said allowing their conversation to come to an end.

"Cool, bye, Miss Baguette. You take care of yourself," he said sounding concerned. He knew something was up. Why would she have to call around looking for Brezell if nothing was wrong? She knew he would not mention to Brezell that she called; he tried not to be in their relationship and definitely didn't ask any questions or state any type of opinion. He pretty much thought Brezell knew better, he knew himself that nobody in John Otis's family was to be fucked over, but unlike Monte, Brezell was proving he did not give a fuck about the policy.

As soon as they ended the call, Chloe's mind was occupied with the fact that he was laid up somewhere with another chick, eating good, most likely fucking good, and who knows what else. She felt too stressed and decided against driving to St. Louis and caught the next thing smoking, a train. Before she got on the train, she stopped at the bookstore and grabbed a few magazines and a book to keep her occupied on the 5-hour ride. It was really 3½ driving, but with all the stops and breaks in between, the ride was extended on a train. She could have easily caught a plane, but decided against it, wanting to have the train ride to clear her mind. She grabbed her lifetime favorite, Cosmo, which kept her up on her sex game and shoe game, a novel called *Victim of the Ghetto* by Joel Rhodes since her man had turned her on to Urban Lit. She didn't usually read books for entertainment purposes, but this form of story telling intrigued her. It was some real live shit the author's were writing.

When her phone finally got some reception, she called to tell Squeak her arrival time and to make sure she would be there on time. She was still at least 2 hours away when she called Squeak. She answered the phone talking like her conversation started before she picked up the phone and was continuing it. Her words just kept flowing like Chloe was in front of her and it continued magically on the phone so she didn't have to stop yapping.

"What? Slow down. Are you talking to me or somebody in the background?" Chloe stated in a more than irritated state.

"I said, Breezy called and asked if you were here yet. Why did you tell him you were coming wit' ya sucka fa' love sick ass?" Squeak chatised, trying to tone down her high pitch voice.

"Did he? And FYI, I didn't tell that nucca anything. He must have talked to my dad. I only told my parents, I swear."

Chloe figured pride would prevent him from calling and asking about her, especially since he was supposed to be so upset with JO.

Humm, I wonder how that came about?, she thought to herself.

"Alright, Squeak, I'll see you in a little bit, I gotta go."

She hung up and couldn't stop letting her thoughts consume her. Many questions filled her head. She wondered what time did Brezell actually come home, how long he waited before searching for her. What his explanation would be for not coming home. She pondered if he tried to call her phone, seeing as how it was roaming for a while. She checked her voicemail and had five messages. The first one was Brezell, the second one, the third, and the fifth all Brezell. The fourth was her mother and father.

Message 1: *What's good? Why the fuck you not answering this phone, get at me, this yo man.*

Message 2: *Girl, you gon make me hurt you, Baguette. Where the fuck is you that you can't answer the damn phone?*

Message 3: *Man, if you don't answer this damn phone, I know you not on no foul shit, girl. For real, quit playing and pick this muthfucka up. I know you see me calling.* In the middle of the message Brezell softened his tone, *Chloe on the real, bay, talk to me. Don't do this to me, stop tripping. Where are you, girl? You really scaring me right now. I don't give a fuck who or what you mad about, you don't disappear and not answer that bitch ass phone, especially 'cause you know what type shit I am on. You know your status out here.*

That third message tickled Chloe at the fact that this nigga couldn't stand to eat the same shit he was serving. She knew for sure his ass was sweating beads, thinking she'd left his ass. She laughed to herself.

Message 4: *Hey baby, this is mommy. Brezell came over looking for you, he was acting a little weird. Why did you lie to us? I thought you said he knew about the 'all girls' trip to St. Louis.*

Diary of a Kingpin's Daughter

What's going on over there with y'all? We need to talk about this later.

Before the message ended, you could hear the sound of Kim passing the phone and JO's voice ended the message.

Baby girl, I forgot to ask you how much you liked New York. New York Cit-taay!!!!! From what I hear, Young Breezy loves it. I'll talk to you when you get back. I love you Chloe, no matter what.

Message 5: *Baby, I know where you're on your way to. Why, baby? Why you gotta try and leave me when my eyes are closed and my back is turned? Please, baby, let's talk this out. Don't make decisions while you're mad. Please, pretty pleazzzze call me. You got a nigga begging and shit. Baguette, you are my diamond; very soon to be my wife, shit is not what you think. I love you, boo, and I'm waiting for you.*

Message 4 made her heart rate change. It was highly noticeable by the sarcasm in her father's voice that he knew something about Brezell doing outside business in New York and he knew Chloe knew something. John Otis only said 'I love you no matter what' when she did something he did not approve of and wanted to let her know he still loved her regardless. When her mind finally returned out of its alienated coma, the train had arrived in St. Louis. Brezell, surprisingly, met her at the baggage check.

His first words to her were, "To be or not to be!"

Chloe frowned in confusion, "To be or not to be, what?" Thinking in her head, 'Dis *nigga is crazy!*

He replied very seriously, "my wife". He hugged Chloe tight, and blew her hair off her ear and whispered, "When I thought you were gone, I couldn't breathe. My world seemed to be closing in on me and I realized I couldn't ever imagine being without you."

Her eyes started burning from trying to hold in all the mixed emotion and uncertainty. Brezell kissed the salty solution running down her face and hugged her firmly whispering, "I'll never hurt you, baby. I'll always be here to catch your tears and drop your pain."

They walked out the train station to a black Caprice with dark tint; nothing could be seen except their reflection. As soon as Brezell opened the door, a heavy cloud of smoke raced out. When the smoked cleared, there sat Squeak and her lover, Jade.

"Hey cuzo," Squeak jumped out and hugged Chloe. During the exchange, she managed to mouth, "I'll explain later."

Chloe played it off and introduced herself to Jade.

"Hey girl, I'm Chloe," she said while extending her hand. Jade rolled her head every time she talked like that's what made out her words.

"Gull, please we fam. Don't shake my hand, you better give me a hug, cuzo. I know who you are."

Jade favored the late Left Eye from the group TLC. She was short, high yellow, and very petite. At a glance, outside from that big badunk-a-dunk bootie, you could mistake her for a teenager. She seemed very crazy~sexy~cool, all in one. She looked like she could have any guy, on any given day, but instead she was madly in love with another woman.

Chloe caught Brezell frowning when she reached out to hug Jade. He, like John Otis, was a homophobic. He switched it with a fake grin when everybody faced him.

"Gull, shawty got it going on!" Jade said annoying the shit out of Brezell, smacking her gum.

"Who?" Squeak and Brezell said in unison.

"Hah ass better be talking bout Chloe. I know this bitch not trying to act like she like dick!" Squeak said in a jealous way.

"Naw, she better be talking bout me and not hitting on my girl while I'm right here!" Both Squeak and Brezell was ready to play mad, waiting on her answer.

Her lil' ghetto ass snapped her fingers like she was writing in thin air and replied in a ghetto Sha-na-nay voice, "Neither one, shit I talking about this little ass 5-year-old girl with a damn Gucci teddy bear and those nice Tiffany Bean earrings I have been trying to get since last month. Damn, a bitch can't compliment a kid without folks getting all insecure and shit?"

Chloe laughed so hard, mainly because Jade was right. Brezell and Squeak tried to laugh it off. *That's what they dog asses get,* she thought to herself.

Without Chloe really recognizing St. Louis, she had no idea where they were headed, but she could read very well. The big, white building the Caprice pulled in front of said "St. Louis County Court House." She turned to ask Brezell what was going on and all she saw was his pearly whites and a platinum 6-carat wedding band with diamonds chasing the ring in a circle. That matched her engagement ring. Chloe stared Brezell down. Before she could speak, he put his finger to her lips to silence her.

"Chloe Baguette Carter, I almost died when I thought I lost you and that was only for a few hours. I can't imagine not being with you the rest of my life. I guess what I'm saying is will you be my wife, right now?"

Chloe kissed the running apology racing from his eyes and replied, "I will never hurt you, baby. I'll always be here to catch your tears and drop your pain."

On June 24th, less than 24 hours after she was so mad at him for not coming home, she became Mrs. Chloe Baguette Carter-Wright in a New York minute.

Diary of a Kingpin's Daughter

Dear Diary,

As usual Brezell made everything better. It's like he hurts me and in the same breath bandages the wounds before I can remember that he caused me harm. I was kind of surprised that he came to St. Louis. I know he loves me but sometimes I think that boys ego and pride is bigger than his heart. In a court room is not exactly how I planned to be married, not at all how I dreamed it up. Daddy is going to kill me that I did it this way... cheating him out of a real lavish wedding. Brezell wasn't taking no for an answer and like he said, it's not like we had to do it 'cause we can't afford a big shindig, 'cause we can. Squeak isn't feeling Brezell like that at all, she said she wish I wasn't so hooked over him.

I called Cashay to tell her our big news. I was puzzled when she asked me if I was sure that I did the right thing. She and Brezell don't really have a tight bond anymore since she's been in college. You would think that would bring them closer since she's gone. But oh well, she acts so distant and is always talking about her new "college" friends.

I tore the malls up shopping away. St. Louis had that shit too. I purposely copped the most expensive stuff. I got a new YSL Muse bag with the matching loafers; I got two pair of Citizen Jeans, three pairs of Sevens, and a few pair of True

Religions. As a wedding gift to Brezell, I got us matching Cartier Love bracelets. I'm still gonna plan my big dream wedding though and maybe we'll go to St. Thomas for our honeymoon. I don't know yet, but I'll let my mother help me decide. I'm so excited to be Mrs. Johnathan Brezell Wright. Can't nobody tell me nothing!

It's ya gurl,

Chloe Baguette Carter-Wright

Vindictive

Two days, and over a few thousand later, the newly weds returned home no longer needing to check single. They were now married; Mr. and Mrs. Jonathan Brezell Wright. They mutually decided not break the news right away, but wait at least a week before they announced their legal document.

Chloe still had a burning desire to ask Brezell where he was the night he did not come home. Although, whatever answer he was going to give wouldn't have made a difference since she was on cloud 9 since saying 'I do.'

"Hey bay, where were you that night? Where did you stay?"

Brezell shifted a bit in his seat. "Me and my dude, BG, took a last minute trip to New York. You know when I'm on business I don't answer the phone. It got late so we crashed a hotel."

And again, Chloe being naïve and in love, that was a good enough excuse for her. Knowing she should have broken out the spy kit on his ass.

"Speaking of New York," she said to Brezell, remembering JO's ironic message. Chloe allowed Brezell to hear the message so he could interpret what he thought it meant himself. Brezell's face was expressionless so it was hard for her to tell if he was shocked, scared, surprised, or had any type of feeling for that matter. He knew as well as she did, John Otis was no punk about his and there was going to be *"Trouble, trouble, Chi-town!"* she mimicked to herself, quoting the character Dollar Bill from Ice Cube's hit movie, *Players Club.*

Instead of responding to what he just heard, Brezell started acting horny, like the message had not fazed him and started kissing her passionately. They made love like it was their first time. He broke out the baby oil gel and rubbed her body down. He started kissing from her forehead and worked his way down to her belly button, gently playing with her navel ring, he blew the spots where he left it wet, purposely causing her to feel chills. When it came to sexing, Brezell knew exactly where the hot spots were. He was so passionate and blessed with a nice package. He slowly nibbled lower and lower, until he had her vaginal lips in his mouth. He sucked, then licked, and at the same time fondled her, going back and fourth until her body started to quiver. Right before her love juices franticly ran down, he stuck his awaiting solidity deep inside of her.

"This my shit, tell me this my good pussy," he moaned and moved rhythmically.

"Yes, Yes, Yessss, this yo kitty, baby, make love to me," she replied to him with her legs in a "Y" shape angle.

"I want you to have my baby, Chloe. Let me give you my seed," he said staring right down at her.

"I wanna have your baby, I'm ready to start our family," she replied staring back at him. Chloe squirmed and grunted, trying to accept all that he was giving her, including his offspring.

"Damn, I love you to death, babe. I never thought it would get like this." Brezell said so innocently. They made love at least 3 more times before he said he had to go handle some business at the pool hall.

"What about daddy's message?" she inquired on his way out the door.

"What about it?" he replied nonchalantly.

"What are we going to say?"

"**WE** ain't gonna say shit 'cause **YOU** don't know what the fuck he's talking about. *I'M* going to call him tomorrow cause he don't know we back and if he knows anything about the connect in NY, I'm going to put it all on Money Green and leave you out of it like you didn't know about nothing," Brezell said with plain expression.

"Damn, baby, that's cold so what you gon say if Monte bring it to you?"

"I'll cross that bridge when I get there. Don't worry your pretty little heart; I'll take care of it."

Damn, he resented Monte that much for being a follower and not a leader, that's cold-blooded. He's the only father he knows, she thought to herself, amazed at how the greed for money could turn you against your own family. And then, she felt really bad because she knew she was part of the mistrust.

Brezell commanded an order before leaving, "Don't call anybody, and don't pick up the fucking phone. I'll take care of it. Love you."

Brezell left quickly leaving her in thought. She did just what he said and did not make any calls or answer any either. It was a perfect time to sleep off their exhausting trip.

▶ ▶ ▶ ▶ ▶

Meanwhile, Brezell was out handling his other business.

"What's good, Go-To, you still babysitting those big, loud, bad ass kids?" Brezell asked Go-To, his gun connect. He learned earlier in the game when you're discussing criminal activity over the phone, you never incriminate yourself.

"Fa sho, my nig, you wanna come get they bad asses!" Go-To responded, happily.

"Yeah, I need the oldest one; I wanna go spoil her to death," Brezell assured.

Go-To didn't ask any questions and understood properly, as he usually did. His motto was: hear no evil, see no evil. It was whatever as long as his burners were getting sold. He had all kind of hustles. You need guns; he got you. You need drugs; he got you. You need clothes; he got you. You need bootleg shit; he got you. You need a few stripper bitches; he got you. Go-To was that "go to" hustling nigga.

"Burn rubber, baby! She's ready," he obliged.

After stopping to see Go-To, Brezell needed to make three more calls before he put his plan into action. First, he called his white guy, Todd "BG" Wedderburn, from the suburb Richton Park, whom he met at the Big Dipper, one of the largest basketball tournaments held each year in Chi. BG wasn't your average white boy; he had more soul than some thugs. If you never seen him and only heard his voice, you would bet the stash, that he was a straight up ghetto dude. They called him BG, short for Baby Gangster, a name that stuck with him since he was 13 when he was the only little white kid in the suburbs selling drugs and gang banging. And this he did by choice because his parents had hella money. BG just wanted to fit in with the in-crowd. He wanted to be down so bad, he would do anything Brezell requested.

"BG, I'm coming through." Brezell informed him.

"What it do, Breezy?" BG answered, very excited.

"It don't do nothing bitch, I'm just coming through to see my nig," Brezell replied acting like BG was one of his favorite comrades. He knew exactly how to manipulate him. "I think my down low ho having a miscarriage and I need about 4, maybe 5 of them dummies to come clean this shit up while I take the no good whore to the emergency room!" Brezell replied once again using his Black Spanish that only he and his people could decipher. In Laymen's terms: *I want to set somebody up to die early, on the down low, but I need 4 maybe 5 of them fake bricks (dope) to make it look like a set up, ASAP!*

"Can I roll with you to the ER, folks?" BG requested, not knowing what he was getting himself into, just wanting to be down with the get down.

"Of course, my nig. That's why I love you 'cause you a straight ride or die nigga, but don't ever call me folks, dawg, I'm not gang related," Brezell stated, happy BG was falling for his master plan. *That was easier than I thought,* he thought to himself.

"My fault, dawg. I just say that since I don't use the 'N' word," BG said hesitantly, hoping he didn't ruin his chances to show his allegiance to a man he looked up to.

"You damn right, nigga. You better not ever use that word or it's gonna be the death of you. Some shit just ain't for white people to say." Brezell cautioned critically, but immediately changed his tone before he busted his plans. "On the real, BG, you the realest white boy I ever met and you got potential, that's why I keep you around. Now get out your feelings white boy, and meet me where they swim at."

Laymen's terms: *Meet me at the pool hall.*

Some of the wealthiest white folks BG knew were the biggest junkies. That's why he kept several bags of the bonafide dope in the event he needed to sell. However, once they sampled the real dope and came back to cop larger amounts, he did the old switch-a-roo getting them for their cash. Many of them didn't have the heart to confront him and those that did were afraid he'd get his black friends to jump up them, so they'd let it slide vowing to never buy from him again. That never stopped BG's hustle though; he'd go city to city selling bad dope.

Brezell made his second call, which was to wifey. For one, to make sure she wasn't answering the phone and for two, to put his alibi in motion. The phone went straight to her voicemail, which made him proud. *Good girl*, he mused to himself. *My baby listens. I got full control of 'dat ass.* He smiled while waiting on the beep to leave her a message on her cell.

"Yeah, you reached the diamond princess, Baguette, love me or hate me, either way speak yo piece... beeeeeeepppp."

"What's really good, Baguette? I was just calling to check on you and tell you I love you till death do us part. Get at me, I'll be down at the pool hall, call me when you wake up."

He pressed 2, to send it as an urgent message so it would be put as priority when she checked her voice mail.

His third call was the most important and he had to be careful not to fuck it up.

"Yeah," the person responded very indifferently on the first ring.

Brezell had to remind myself, once again, he couldn't fuck this up, so held in his urging smart remark for the time being, all the while thinking, *A nigga on the come up and bitch niggas always get jealous.*

It was all good because Brezell knew he would get the last laugh, so he kept his composure and replied, "What up folks," with emphasis, knowing he didn't talk like that. "I need to holler at you bout them thangs!"

The person on the other end of the phone automatically knew what he was talking about cause he wanted to holler at Brezell about them "thangs" as well.

"Well, when I get back in, I'll hit you 'cause I'm already in motion. Plus, I'm with company," he responded.

Brezell was too impatient and needed to handle this business right away so he had to throw a curve ball.

"You might wanna get at me pronto, mi amigo," he patronized. Brezell laughed at his own wit. "It's important." He pleaded with the man in a cynical way.

Going against his plans, the guy decided to swing his way.

BG entered the pool hall in search of Brezell. Since he was so well known around the spot he was allowed in the back where the city's major playa's gambled. Not petty shit either, they gambled real shit at stake – rental properties, cars, jewels, and sometimes even women. Nobody was bothered at the fact that this white boy was fading their spot because everybody knew he was worth a million on the low. When he couldn't find Brezell, he went back in his car and phoned him.

"What up, Breezy? I'm at the pool, man, and I don't see you swimming nowhere," BG admonished, sitting in his white G-wagon Benz with custom-made black leather seats, black carpeting and chromed the fuck out.

"Nigga, change of plans. Come to Ford Heights, behind the old roller rink, and make sure don't nobody follow yo ass," Brezell demanded, smirking to himself, ready to put his plan into action. "I hope you got ya shawty wit' you and my bag of goodies," he referenced, referring to BG bringing his gun and the fake cook up.

"Fa sho, my dude," BG replied in his best version of Ebonics.

When BG pulled up behind the gigantic skating rink, he only saw one vehicle with three occupants. He immediately accompanied Brezell in the back seat of the all-black BMW M5 sports car.

"Quit looking stupid, nigga, and give me what I asked for," he yelled at BG.

"'Nough respect, JO. How you doo-ii-ng Mrs. JO?" BG stuttered, to the silent driver and passenger of the SUV, hoping the response would relieve him of his worst fear, that the King and Queen of the hood weren't the fatalities.

When neither one of them responded, BG knew right then his ass had bitten off more than he could chew, but it was too late.

"Fool ass nigga, did I tell you to speak to anybody?" Brezell shouted furiously. "Ohh yeah, I know what you're thinking too!" He added sarcastically while spitting out the window. Brezell thoughts frantically ran rapid.

"What are you talking about, bro?" BG responded in a nervous and regretful way.

"You thinking what da fuck is up? I ain't dumb bitch!" And without BG responding, but looking bewildered, Brezell pointed the silencer that he snatched from JO and shot him.

In attempt to fight back, BG grabbed for Brezell's face, causing a small scratch above his eyebrow, which pissed Brezell off even more. He was gonna shoot him in the head, but aimed for his eye in close range instead causing part of BG's brains to splatter on the window.

Brezell wiped the dripping blood from his scratch and continued his mission. Kim began to vomit and urinate on herself at the same time out of fear.

Without blinking, he shot Kim, his "supposed" loving mother-in-law, in the back of the head with the gun BG had in his waistline causing her body to slump to the dashboard.

JO scrambled to shield her but it all happened to fast. "Noooo!!!" He shrieked in a high pitch tone from the depths of his tunnel.

"What you got to say now, ho ass nigga!" Brezell shouted violently to John Otis causing the tears that sat in the corner of JO's eyes to fall.

"Why, nigga, why? I just want to know why you would betray me like this." JO wept from the sight of his slumped queen. "I gave my daughter to you. I took your mother and father under my wing. I groomed you and ya sister's homey ass and this is how you play me?

"Why what? Cry baby ass nigga! Why my dick tastes so good in your daughter's mouth or why the fuck you can't own up to your responsibilities?" Brezell answered in rage, knowing the meaning to the second question wouldn't register to him right away.

"I'll tell you what, ask me again when I meet you in hell!" he yelled, clinching his jaw as he often did out of habit.

Again without hesitation, Brezell pointed at a still JO who stared at him without the fear of death.

"Look me in the eyes you bitch ass nigga when you kill me. Be a real man about ya shit. You punk ass mothafucka! You can't fade a nigga like JO. I knew you always wanted ya daddy to be like me. I can't help that didn't happen. I always knew you wanted me to be ya daddy, but I wasn't mothafucka! And nigga, ya dick might taste good in my daughter's mouth, but I'm sure my dick tasted sweeter in Tina's. That mouth, pussy, and ass was mmm, mmm, good, nigga! Ya momma knew how to treat a nigga *real good*." JO laughed and continued staring down at a startled Brezell. "You lil' soft ass wanna-be JO nigga, die a slow death, bitch!"

Tears of embarrassment boiled in Brezell's eyes as he shot in hatred at JO, killing him with BG's gun.

Careful not to leave any fingerprints, Brezell kept his leather gloves on before planting the stack of fake bricks and Go-To's silencer in JO's lap. He sat the bag of money in BG's lap and placed BG's gun in his hand.

Brezell left the scene feeling confident it would be ruled a botched drug deal transaction turned deadly. Although taunted by his mother's death, he still felt a rush of power playing God. He didn't feel a bit of sorrow and was not bothered by death. Instead, he thought greedily about the large inheritance he knew Chloe had coming and his new mission was to convince her to give him full access to the funds.

It was undisputable; Brezell would now be the new H.N.I.C.! And if this was the way he had to do it, so be it.

One monkey don't stop the show

Brezell let the hot water wash away his sins at one of his side bitch's crib, less than twenty minutes after he had just played God. He felt the power of a king given that he'd taken three lives. It was his time to step up and run shit, so it was inevitable that blood would be shed.

Who would be next in line? Who other than me? Sho' in fuck not Money's weak, flunky ass!, he grimed to himself. He threw on an almost identical outfit that he left the house in four hours prior. He had a few outfits at his number two bitch's house for his convenience. Most of the time, he was a simple dude, not that flashy; not with clothes anyway. Jewelry and cars was another story. He only got so fresh and so clean when he was going somewhere and felt he had to let people know he was that nigga. So on a regular, everyday basis, he kept it straight hood. Nike Airs, a crispy white tee, jeans, and on occasion, Gucci sneaks. His jewelry made his t-shirt look like a different get-up everyday, although it was always a new white tee and some jeans accented with his white-on-white Nikes. He had a custom-made chain that had a huge diamond-filled letter "B" with the letter "C" facing the opposite way like the Chanel symbol. Every time he would catch Chloe staring at it, he would hold it up, reflecting the light and tell her, "We Bonnie and Clyde, baby." When, really, it stood for Brezell and Chloe. He had her in her feelings about a nigga; she breathed him.

Without the dame knowing he was throwing away evidence, Brezell discarded his murder outfit in the dumpster outside of her apartment. When he came back in she was all in his face.

"Damn, nigga, you got it like that where you can throw away outfits after one wear? Can a bitch get some Similac money?" the girl's voice grilled with much attitude.

"See, there you go with that bullshit and you wonder why a nigga don't never wanna stay around this muthfucka cause all the fuck you do is nag, damn!"

"I'm not nagging, I'm just saying, you throwing shit away like it's nothing and I got to sweat the shit out of you for pamper money! Like, what the fuck is that? I bet you Chloe don't want for nothin'. What's that about? I have your child."

"Don't even go there, that's cause yo ass be trying to be slick," Brezell said, offended by her comment. "Don't try and make it like I'm some type of deadbeat, that's not even how it's going down," he retorted.

"Yeah, you play your part, but you are on that ole, 'If I see something my son need, I'll get it myself' type shit. Why I can't shop for *our* son sometimes? I see stuff I want him to have and then when I tell you about it, you only get it if you feel like *you* want him to have it," she said disappointed.

"That's 'cause when I let money touch your hands, you either shopping for yourself or on that damn gamble boat and then want to come back to me like I didn't give you enough. You got life and bullshit all fucked up," he grinned.

The girl just smiled, "Fuck you, nigga, you don't know me like that."

They both laughed.

"Go get my son so I can see him before I leave; I gotta go." He smacked her wide ass before she walked next door to get the baby.

"Don't you always gotta go," she grunted, sucking her teeth.

She returned right away with her two fingers in the palm of a 2-year-old's hand. As soon as the child walked through the door, his face lit up when he saw Brezell's familiar face looking down on him with the same eyes as his. His little man was his soft spot, probably the only person that he loved for real.

Brezell picked up his mini me, calling him by his nickname, "What up J-dub?" he said lifting his little boy in the air.

"Dah-dee," the little boy chimed.

"We be missing you," the girl whined speaking for her and the baby.

"We, huh?" he said looking at the girl with a smirk.

"Yeah, nigga, we," she replied, in a soft voice.

Brezell tried to show some compassion; he held her close to him with one arm and his son in the other.

"Be cool, baby, daddy coming home and we gone be a family, just like you want, watch," he said to her with true sincerity.

"But when, Brezell? I've been watching for years now, so when? That line is getting old."

"The shit I'm on, you wouldn't understand. I'm just gone handle my business, then we relocating up out this muthafucka, and we gone start our new life. Our family in another area code, you feel me." Brezell felt bad, but he had to bounce, he still had shit to take care of. Handing her the baby and a fat knot of money, he kissed her forehead and headed for the door. "You know I love you," he said to her, and afterwards kissed his baby, "love you too, lil' man." He turned to walk out, "Baby, I got to go, where my keys."

Brezell knew that money would cure her attitude and each time he gave it to her in large amounts, it bought her more time to wait for the relationship she yearned to have with him. He knew she wouldn't stop at anything until she got what she wanted and that was for them to become a family, but the mistress act was growing old.

Less than an hour after catching three bodies, Brezell walked in the pool hall, speaking to somebody every two steps. Everybody spoke to him and those who didn't notice him he spoke to them anyway just to be noticed. He wanted it be known he was in the pool hall; it would serve as his official alibi. He knew if he hung out at the pool hall for a strong minute people would vouch for him. There was no telling when somebody was going to notice the bodies laying in back of the building. It was a no trespassing area. Unless somebody else was on some grimy shit, it would be a while before the bodies were found.

▶ ▶ ▶ ▶ ▶

Chloe finally woke up after what seemed like hours of sleep. She automatically called the pool hall to see if that's where Brezell really was. He had been caught up with that line so many times before, only disclosing that he had lied about his whereabouts. She had the number on speed dial, saved as *1 and "pool," which would appear on her screen as it dialed instantly. Juan, one of JO's lieutenant's, answered the phone when she called. As usual, she asked for him which, Juan always hated, but he didn't want to be disrespectful so whether he knew if Brezell was there or not, he would always reply, "Let me check." If he was there, he would let him know, "Wifey on the phone, what you want me to tell her?"

Most of the time Brezell would come to the phone; other times, he'd tell him to tell her, he was busy. If Brezell was ghost, just to keep it neutral, sure not to bust him out, Juan would say, "I just saw him, he might be in the back yard," he would lie, referring to the gamble room. That way he never said if he was there, but he also never said he wasn't.

This time fortunately, Brezell came to the phone.

"What up I-spy 007?" he answered, laughing at Chloe trying to play detective.

"Hey, baby, what you doing?" she gleamed back not ashamed at trying to catch him up.

"Nothing. Came down here to handle some business and ended up kickin' it for about four hours shooting pool. What, you just got up?"

"Yep," she said yawning.

"Alright, I'll be there so we can order some food, watch a movie, and go over what we gonna say to ya daddy when we talk to him," he said, playing devil's advocate.

"Oh, now it's *we*," she smacked her lips.

"Naw, I just need you to back me up, nah mean."

"Alright, Mr. Breezy, see you in minute," Chloe replied playfully.

"Cool, call ya momma and act like we just got back, but act like you real tired and say you gonna call her in the morning. Tell her we should all go to lunch or something," he recommended.

"Okay, I'll do that now," Chloe responded, going along with his plan.

As soon as Chloe hung up with Brezell, she called her mom, but got her voicemail.

"Hey, Mrs. John Otis, I was calling to let you know I'm back and to see if you and daddy wanted to join me and Brezell for lunch. What you doing that you can't answer this phone anyway? Just playing, but for real, call me tomorrow. I'm about to go to bed, I'm bushed from that ride talk to you later. I love you mommy."

Later on, Brezell walked into their loft like it was a normal night and immediately, he was greeted at the door by the scent of his wife's Creed for Women perfumed body gel. His dick hardened just thinking about her soapy body in the shower. He walked in the bathroom ass naked startling her. Of course she relaxed when she realized it was her husband. He joined her in their all-glass shower.

"Damn, I love the way that smells," he said, referring to the scent of the body gel. "I'mma buy you a lifetime supply of that shit," he said cheesing.

"Babe, you so silly, you always say that." She gleamed happy he was home with her and not running the streets as usual.

Brezell knew for a fact, he made his wife feel safe and secure. She often told him that his touch was comforting to her. Glancing at the clock radio they had mounted on the shower wall, only 12:00 p.m. He was home early.

Chloe closed her eyes as he kissed her wet skin softly, massaging certain areas gently with his teeth.

"Are you in the house for good or are you here to chill for a hot minute and be back out?" she asked frustrated, with her eyes still closed.

On a normal day, Brezell would have japed out about her not being satisfied with the time she was getting, but tonight was different; he knew bad news was coming to devastate her and he wanted to be right there under her to play savior of her sorrow.

"I'mma stay here with my Baguette," he said in between kisses. He stood up straight and held the sides of her face, positioning their noses close. She opened her eyes and their eyes locked. "Baby, things are about to change around here. We married now, bay, it's all about you from now on. If you say you wanna go to the mall, we there; to the movies, we there. Shit, I was even thinking about starting to go to church with you; it's whatever you want, I promise," he said very sincere.

"I love you, babe. I swear to God, I love you, and I want us to be together forever," she said with tears in her eyes.

"Sometimes, I think I love you more than I love myself," he said allowing his emotions to ride with hers. "On the real, I feel the same way. I often smile at you, thinking, 'I love this girl more than life itself'." He charmed her while closing her eyes and kissing her eyelids. "We're gonna be together forever, till death do us part," he confessed, pulling her left eyebrow gently between my lips. "And baby, later we need to discuss getting joint accounts. We are one in every way now."

Gently picking up her petite frame and wrapping her legs around his waist, Brezell leaned Chloe against the cold tile and pushed himself inside of her. Their hearts beat at the same pace. Chloe gripped his neck tightly and tried to join the flow of his rhythm.

"Throw it back." Brezell huffed in between strokes. He stepped out the shower with her still clinging to his waist and laid her out on their king sized bed. He placed one of her legs on his shoulder and continued to make love to her. He looked down at her as she laid there with her eyes closed making sex faces and he almost felt bad. Falling in love with her so deeply was never part of the plan. The arrangement was to use her to get closer to her father to seek revenge.

Evil thoughts instantly started crossing his mind and with each thought, he pumped harder and harder. She was looking at him with terror in his eyes as she looked into his face and saw a disgruntled expression occupy it.

"Stop, baby, stop, you're hurting me. Brezell, stop!" she squalled from under him. He didn't pay attention to her pleas; he just kept thrusting harder and harder, until he collapsed, eyes full of tears. To Brezell, he was just plain ole fucked up about his mother's death and often had mood swings about her death.

Tina was so severely depressed and her diagnosis of Bi-polar with meds still didn't help. It was fucked up how Brezell found her limp body lying across her bed with her diary next to her, along with a bottle of sleeping pills, and a bottle of cognac. He never told anybody about the diary other than Chloe. From her diary, Brezell learned of the secret affair she had with JO. Tina wrote how she longed to be with John Otis and not Monte, the fake ass nigga. Brezell unlocked many confessions when he read her diary. Tiny wrote about her deep depression and if JO wouldn't leave Kim, she would kill herself. Ultimately, Tina lost the battle with her love and illness. And Brezell blamed John Otis for her death.

When Chloe noticed the tears, she automatically forgot about her own pain. "What's wrong, baby?" she asked in a concerned voice. At first, Brezell just nodded his head until he could think of something to replace his evil flashbacks.

"I love you so much that I started to think of you giving your love to somebody else the way you give it to me and I got upset. I'm sorry, I couldn't control myself." He lied still feeling the anger from his thoughts. She held him in her arms and rubbed his back until she felt him begin to release the tense state he was in.

"I promise you, I'll never love another like I love you. I'll never share my love with anybody like I do you. I am your Baguette, baby. Your flawless diamond. I'll never hurt you, I'm here to catch your tears and drop your pain."

Brezell looked into her eyes and saw truth in her words. She loved him with all the energy she had in her. Their tears united and they drifted to sleep in each other's arms through the night.

Damn, I fucked up. I wish it didn't have to do it like this; she actually loves me, Brezell thought to himself, falling into a deep sleep.

Dear Diary,

This is my first time coming to you as Chloe Baguette Carter-Wright. I'm going to break the news to mommy and daddy real soon. I know daddy is going to be pissed off. We still plan to have a big wedding with all our family and friends, but Brezell said he couldn't wait.

I don't know what daddy knows about New York, but I figured it couldn't be too much cause if he knew exactly what type of connect Brezell had in New York, he wouldn't be this patient, he would've handled it with Brezell ASAP. I don't know, but we shall find out soon.

Brezell made love to me. Well, at first it started off making love, but then he went into this rage; he was beating it up for real, for real. Not like our passionate break-up to make-up sex when he calls himself putting it down, but more like he was really trying to hurt me. He had this deranged look on his face almost like it wasn't him and then he fell out in tears. I wanna talk to him about it, but I don't know how to bring it up without embarrassing him. This is the second time he went into a weird episode like that. I can't explain it, but I know it's not normal. He blames it on his insecurities. I do all that I can to show him how much I love him, but yet still he has doubts. I wonder if there is anything else I can do. Whatever it is, without hesitation, it's done. He also asked me about a joint account, but I'm not sure about *that. Brezell doesn't know exactly what I'm worth; I got true money at stake, but I am willing to share it with my baby.*

I need to talk to mommy; I can't wait to ask her if she's ready to be a grandmother. I can already imagine what she gone say, "I'm too young to be a grandma." Well, she better start getting old, 'cause I'm ready to be a mother.

It's ya girl,

Chloe Baguette Carter-Wright

Nothing good about this morning

The morning didn't start off normal at all. In fact, it started off in mourning. A rainy, summer morning in June and peaceful dreams came to a halt by loud thumps on the door. Chloe dreamt of her childhood when she and JO had daddy/daughter day. They used to do that every Saturday morning, when it would just be the two of them.

"Ready for our date?" he would say.

"Ready when you are, daddy."

It felt so good to see him smiling down on her; he was so overjoyed to have her in his life. She felt herself smiling in her sleep. She lit up like a glowworm every time he ended a call quickly telling the caller, "I'll have to get back with you, I'm on a date with my daughter. You're on her time right now."

Chloe could smell the scent of his car in her dream; the fresh leather smell, the air freshener, and the new car scent. They would ride and talk for hours about anything and everything; going wherever she requested. This was their bonding time. This was a reoccurring dream for her. Her cheeks hurt from smiling so hard. Only this time, the dream didn't have the same ending with her falling asleep on the ride home after their long day together.

"Watch out, daddy!" Chloe screamed in her dream as the car swerved trying to avoid being hit by a truck. That dream was ended by the continuous loud bangs on the door. Chloe jumped up in a cold sweat and Brezell was already up, searching for his boxers.

"What were you dreaming about?" he asked taking his time to put on his boxers.

"Who's at the door?" she questioned now searching for her robe. She stood at the top of the stairs as Brezell proceeded to find out who was beating on the door like a crazy person.

"Who the fuck is it?" he shouted, peeking through the peephole. He saw Aunt Ryan standing there in frenzy ready to begin pounding again if somebody didn't open the door immediately. As soon as Brezell opened the door, Aunt Ryan rushed in rambling.

"Baby girl, I've been calling you all morning, but your phone is off!" she stated in a nervous panic.

Fuck! I forgot I had turned my power back off after Brezell said he was on his way home, Chloe regretted to silently.

"What's up?" Brezell asked. When their eyes met, she saw it and she already knew what this surprise visit was for. She read it in her aunt's eyes and felt it in her heart; she just knew. Kim had taught her well about the game. Before Aunt Ryan could speak, Chloe fell to the floor.

No, it's okay, mommy and daddy are okay, she told herself over and over again, already in tears. Ryan came to the top of the stairs and embraced her, rocking back and fourth.

"Chloe, I got a call that a crackhead found JO and Kim this morning, dead! Somebody shot them, baby. They're gone." Her voice cracked with each word.

Ryan held Chloe as she curled up like a baby. Her body froze up with those words; she could no longer feel her existence. Brezell spoke, but she couldn't hear him, his mouth was in a silent motion. She couldn't feel her aunt's clinch anymore. Her vision seemed as though someone had blind folded her or knocked her out. Her body was still at the top of the stairs, now in the arms of Brezell, but her inner being felt as though someone kidnapped it; the ransom was the life of her parents. Chloe fainted.

They had to do something and something fast so they fast tracked to the hospital.

Chloe was awakened by a strong smell that caused a burning sensation to her nose. She blinked several times to gain focus on the images in front of her. Brezell stood over her fanning while a nurse called for a doctor.

"She's up," the nurse stated through the small intercom.

"Baby," Brezell exhaled, kissing her forehead.

Chloe sat there looking confused as she attempted to study the room. Ryan sat in the corner of the room, her eyes bloodshot red with a look of distress. The words of Ryan visited her again as she came to the conclusion she was in a hospital bed. Her chest started to feel tight; it felt like she was chasing her last breath as her heart rate increased. The monitor that was attached to her chest started beeping as it showed lines moving up and down in a fast pace.

"Breathe, calm down and breath; relax, and breathe," the nurse instructed Chloe as Brezell started fanning her again.

"Don't do this to me. I need you, just breathe." Brezell joined in the attempt to calm her down.

"Where's my mother and father?" she began to scream hysterically. The nurse pulled a needle out of her uniform pocket and injected it into the IV.

"Your mouth will feel a little salty," she warned patting Chloe's shoulder. After a few minutes, her body unwillingly relaxed as her state calmed.

Brezell held her hand and spoke, "Baguette, I'm here, baby; it's going to be okay."

Ryan stood on the other side of the bed holding her other hand as she cried uncontrollably. Words were unable to escape her mouth; her vocal cords felt as though they had been stolen. Tears rolled down her pale face as the thought of living without her parents pierced her heart. The medicine not only relaxed her helped her sleep without interruption.

Later, Chloe awoke to muffled voices. The doctor explained her medications to Brezell and Ryan as he prepared for Chloe's release.

"Do you think she's suicidal?" The doctor asked, going over a checklist.

"No," Brezell replied.

"Okay. If she has another black-out or anxiety bout, to relax her, you should give her these." It was a prescription of Valium to help relax her and a bottle of anti-depressants to help stabilize her mood. "Chloe experienced a panic attack; give her one, no more than two each daily of either medication and follow up with her regular doctor one week from today," the small-framed, male doctor explained approaching the bed Chloe occupied in a fetal position. "Mrs. Wright, you're going to be okay," he stated, patting her on her legs. Chloe didn't bother to respond.

I'll never be okay, my life is over, I can't live without my whole heart, she mourned silently.

"Do you feel like you might harm yourself or others?" He questioned with his stethoscope now to her chest. She barely shook her head no. The doctor turned to walk away handing Brezell the signed discharge papers and prescriptions. After which, he carelessly exited the room.

▶ ▶ ▶ ▶ ▶

Unbeknown to Brezell, two floors up lay BG in a coma, holding on for dear life. If God decided to spare his life, the chances of him ever being normal again were slim to none. His brain fought hard to maintain its natural state.

▶ ▶ ▶ ▶ ▶

At home, things would never be back to the usual, but it was as standard as ordinary would ever get since the demoralizing news. Aunt Ryan, Squeak, and Chloe put together all of the funeral arrangements.

"Set everything up; whatever the cost. I got it, they were my family, too," Brezell sensationalized, trying to comfort his wife. "The streets talk and as soon as I get word of who was behind this, I'm gone handle it; don't you worry, baby, I'm gon' make John Otis proud."

A double funeral was held for JO and Kim. Their coffins were fit for royalty, pearl white fiberglass. The inside of Kim's coffin was a soft pink satin and JO's was platinum satin.

The wake was crowded; packed wall-to-wall like a happening club and, with no respect for the dead, some of the people attending came like that's exactly where they were going afterwards. One chick came in there with a black halter mini dress that drooped in the front, half showing her ass, and some 4-inch stilettos on; talk about a hot ass mess. Nigga's had on bandanas and gang paraphernalia, ghetto fabulous, straight out the p-j's. Women with little kids cried out to their alleged baby's daddy, their alleged man, and provider. It was bananas.

Things were like a blur to Chloe, a bad dream. All she wanted was for all of this to be over, to wake up, and her parents would be alive. Everybody was coming up to her talking about how things would be all right and if she needed anything, they got it. Everybody had good things to say about John Otis. Half of them couldn't even put together a complete sentence. They spoke in Ebonics, broken English and mispronounced words. Regardless of their background, age, religion, or education, JO helped them out in some type of form or fashion. The newspapers labeled him the modern day savior.

A 14-year-old, 6th grade dropout stood in front of the podium ready to give his last respects to a man he admired. He had the body of a little boy, but the stress and face of a wary old man.

"Udally," he said, mispronouncing the word usually, "I would'na got in front of alota people like dis, but dat man right dere," he stated pointing at JO's coffin. "He helped me. He da only one dat showed me love when my momma hit da screets and left me, and my little sister alone, to go off an' smoke da rent money. When I told JO we was hungry, dat man right dere made sure we ate erryday, you feel me. Wasn't no momma, no daddy, no family, just me and my little sister doing bad." The young boy held his face to hide his tears before proceeding. "Thank you JO. I never told you, but I loveded you, man." He walked back to his seat with his hands concealing his face.

After that, so many people lined up to say their last respects.

The funeral staff had to limit everybody's comments to two minutes or less. Eventually, they had to stop letting people in the door because it became overcrowded. Passing by, you would have thought it was an event going on, some type of convention. People were outside selling t-shirts with pictures of John Otis on the front. Some wanted to get in so bad, they offered to pay at the door, and to top it all off, dope heads were outside trying to sell the obituary to go get a quick fix. The shit was chaotic. Through all of the chaos, Chloe sat strong; at least it appeared that way on the outside. She was now addicted to the Valiums the doctor had prescribed a week earlier. She had completely lost her appetite and started sleeping the days away. This was the beginning of her nervous break down. Her parents were not the only one's that died, she died as well, but hers was a mental demise.

Villain in disguise

For days, weeks, and months, Chloe shut the world out. She spoke to her Aunt Ryan and Squeak every few days just to prevent frequent pop-up visits and back-to-back calls. Squeak was so worried about her favorite cousin that she was planning to move back to Chicago just to be closer to her. Squeak and Jade drove up almost every weekend to check on her before the complete move.

Brezell and Chloe seemed very distant now. His trips to New York became more frequent, only now she refused to accompany him. Brezell went on as if nothing ever happened. He would get aggravated with her and her constant crying and indirect way of starving herself.

"Baby, you need to eat, you starting to look sick. Chloe, death is a part of life. You act like you ain't got me and we ain't got each other. My momma gone, too! I ain't got a real daddy and you don't see me giving up on the world." He would often repeat the same speech before leaving her for days at a time.

To Chloe, Brezell had no emotion towards her extreme loss. Lately, his main concern was her meeting with her parent's lawyer to sign for her inheritance. To him, she was overdoing it by allowing the deaths to take a major toll on her life. What he didn't understand was that she felt guilty and mad at herself. She never got a chance to tell her mom and dad she had gotten married, never told her mom she was ready for a baby of her own. She felt especially bad that she kept secrets from her father, something she rarely did. To her, life would never be the same. Every time she closed her eyes she heard JO's strong laugh, smelled his scent, and remembered his shadow. She could remember Kim braiding her hair and painting their nails. She could still hear John Otis tell her, "Don't put polish on my baby's nails." but Kim did it anyway.

What do I do now, how do I go on with out them... the right and left side of my heart? I've never known of anybody surviving without theirs. It's not possible; I just want to die to be with my family again, she mourned daily, slowly destroying her will to live. Suicide crossed her mind frequently.

Dear Diary,

    I wish I were dead. I want to be with my family. I contemplate suicide, but I'm too afraid to hurt myself. I just wish God would do me a favor and take me in my sleep. I feel like I'm all alone. Everyday, my husband becomes a stranger to me. He shows no sympathy for my sorrow. The police stopped the investigation on the deaths because they found drugs and unregistered guns. Every thought I have is of my family and our life, which is no more. Why did this have to happen to me, why now? Sometimes I feel like this is one big, bad dream. I feel partially responsible for the deaths, like it's my fault. If only I was not in St. Louis, not being so selfish. Not putting my all into Brezell.

    Please God, give me the strength to change the things that are unacceptable and accept the things that are unchangeable. Help me at my time of need. In your son, Jesus' name, AMEN.

It's ya girl,

Chloe Baguette Carter-Wright

Fallen

It had been three days since Chloe had seen Brezell and it seemed like forever since she last ate. She didn't even attempt to call and find out where her husband was. To keep it real, she didn't care. In fact, at times his presence annoyed the hell out of her. His constant mention of her parent's estate and the large trust they left for her, had her thinking Brezell was more concerned about the money involved.

It had to be about 8 o'clock in the morning when Brezell burst through the doors of their room, where she slept on the chaise, at the edge of their bed. Brezell sat her straight up, trying to get her full attention. His smile warmed her skin and comforted her heart this time. She knew she was hallucinating, but she saw her father in Brezell's image. She elatedly wrapped her arms around him tightly and almost knocked the cup he was holding out of his hand.

"Slow down, boo, I'm not going anywhere!" he chuckled a deep laugh and again she thought she heard her father's laughter. She inhaled his scent and smelled JO's fumes in her mind.

Chloe was enthralled in a figment of her imagination. She was snapped out of her daze when the hot liquid kissed her lips and mixed in with her saliva. Brezell baby-fed her chicken noodle soup.

By Lenaise Meyeil

"Baguette, please eat. You are starting to get skinny." Brezell pushed a straw into her mouth. Chloe felt weak and fatigued and decided to allow Brezell to revive her.

After feeding her, Brezell ran some bath water, placed her in the tub, and bathed her like a newborn. He then placed her toothbrush in her hand and watched her brush her teeth.

"What day is it?" she asked, clearing her rusty vocal cords.

"Today is Thursday, August 9th the day you will learn to live again." Brezell helped her get dressed, hoping she would return to body and spirit. "Here, take this, it will help," he said handing her a large white pill. "Oh, I almost forgot," he said turning to walk out the room, returning with an inspirational book by Iyanla Vanzant. "Here, read this. It somewhat helped my mom when she was down."

He helped Chloe get dressed and lead her to the car. She didn't ask any questions, and just followed his lead.

One Day My Soul Just Opened Up, she read the title to the book silently, ready to read herself to recovery. Twenty minutes later and 2 pills better, the two of them were in front of her favorite spot, well second favorite – the spa. Brezell paid for the ultimate deluxe treatment. They were pampered for at least two and a half hours. They talked and ate strawberries and drank Champagne as part of his planned therapy.

Of course, it didn't make her get over the fact that her parents were gone and never coming back, but along with Brezell, Mrs. Vanzant, and a milk bath, living didn't seem that bad after all.

After the spa, Brezell had to go handle some business so he dropped her off at the hair shop, Split Endz, owned by one of her childhood friends, Karma. It was rumored that Karma was one of JO's young mistresses and the shop was purchased as a hush technique. Chloe never questioned it; in fact, she really didn't want to know.

Karma had it going on, she was the daughter of one of the flyest older chicks in the area, Komara. Komara treated Karma like her little sister instead of a daughter since she had her when she was 13-years-old. She didn't want a big 5-year-old to holler, "Momma," to a young, up and coming 18-year-old, so Karma called her mother by her first name. Karma, standing barely at 5'0", was a feisty, half-white, half-black, and Philippine young woman with an old soul. To sit and talk to Karma was like talking to a woman with many years lived. Chloe loved to talk to her. Karma seemed to always keep it real, but was also very informative and to think that she was only months older than her was astonishing. At the ripe age of 20, she lived the life of a well-experienced 35-year-old as far as experience and knowledge. She was very attractive to say the least; she put you in mind of a ghetto version of Halle Berry.

"What's up bia-atch!" Karma shouted when Chloe walked through the door. "I know you got all those messages I left yo ass about my sympathy."

Chloe had to stop her from bombarding her with words before she got teary eyed again. "Yeah, yeah, yeah, but the real issue is can you squeeze me in without an appointment?"

"Fa sho, you know you VIP around this ho," she said giving her a tight squeeze.

The shop was off the hook. Each station's mirror was shaped like a Medusa head, the face was the mirror and what would be snakes coming from the head were designed into the wall. The shop was raw business, designed by the infamous mother and daughter team, Komara and Karma. Chloe didn't get her usual body wrap, she decided to go with some twists to the back going into a bun for convenience of a head wrap and oil sheen. She promised to call Karma as soon as possible, especially since she claimed to have so much to tell her. She put emphasis on that. Chloe had no intentions on calling her. She wasn't nearly ready for all the gossip Karma would spew.

▶ ▶ ▶ ▶ ▶

Ring, Ring, Ring! Brezell's cell phone begged to be answered from the constant ringing.

"I gotta go, wifey is ready. Sho koops blowing up my phone," he said, searching for his other shoe.

"It's over there." The girl pointed towards the shoe and smacked her lips with much attitude. "I'm so tired of this back and forth shit, I'll still fly to NY for you, but you need to just gone and stay over there with her, let me live my life, and let me find my baby a step daddy."

Before he knew it, Brezell had the girl pinned down by her hair. "Slut, don't play with me. You mine, I own you. Let me find out you got a nigga over here playing daddy to my son, I promise you, I'll kill you and that nigga," he said with rage.

"I'm sorry, I'm sorry, please, I was just joking," the girl cried out in pain as he gripped tighter.

"Now tell me you're mine!" he demanded. The girl cried in torture as she felt strands of her hair being pulled from her scalp.

"Brezell, I love you, your son loves you. We just want you to come home for once and stay. You're all I want, you're all I think about, and I'd do anything to have you to myself," the girl said, bawling in tears. In his twisted mind, the sign of pain gave him pleasure. He loosened his grip on her head and guided it towards his now hardened dick.

"Show daddy how much you love him," Brezell said with a sinister look.

In obedience, she obeyed and unzipped his size 36 jeans and went to work like her life depended on it. Not because she was scared, but because she knew this was the only power she had over him; her notorious blowjob skills. Damn, she had a mean head game. The veins in his dick pulsated to her every stroke. The best mouth work in the hood.

Now I know why I keep this ho around, he thought to himself frozen in gratification. "AWWW, AWW, shitttt, AWWW, I'm about to cum!" he warned her as she stroked with both hands, using lots of spit, right on point, just how he loved it.

Without warning, she stopped.

"What the fuck you stopping for?" Brezell asked enslaved in her oral duties.

She teased the head of his dick with her warm tongue.

"Say my name and tell me you love me," she said with a childish grin as she began to hypnotize his manhood once again, getting ready for his cum to plaster her tonsils.

"I love you, girl."

"Nah nigga, say my name!"

Going along with it, Brezell muffled out, "AWWW shit, B... Bi... onca, Bionca, you know I love you. Damn, B, why you gotta do me like this?"

Her tongue deed would bring any man doubling back. It had him coming back for years, even planting a seed in Bionca early on. The son that Chloe once wanted to become a "TT" to was in fact, her husband's second son on her – Johnson Bryant Wright, bka "J-dub".

A made man

With home back in order, it was time for Brezell to get shit right on the streets and claim his throne. He knew without John Otis, niggas wasn't making any moves. JO hand-fed and supplied most of the major hustlers in the city who was making money. Brezell knew his only challenge would be his father. Brezell had it set in his mind that he would go as far as killing Monte if need be. He also felt that the police didn't care about another hustler found slain; it was helping them clean up the streets.

One less drug dealer to arrest, he thought with treachery in his mind they would say.

"You ready?" Monte asked unlocking the doors to his Porsche truck.

"Yeah, I'm riding with you, pops." Brezell stated, heading towards the vehicle. The two of them planned to have lunch at one of Brezell's favorite restaurants; Grand Lux. Brezell could hardly wait until the waitress put the menu down before getting right to the point of this meeting. They sat extra close to the exit, both being careful of each other in case one was wired. Not that either of them seriously suspected each other, but after John Otis's assassination, the game was all fucked up; nobody was to be trusted, not even each other. It's not like Brezell gave a fuck, he didn't care; he made it that way in the first place.

"A nigga still need to eat, what up with John Otis' connect?" he asked mixed in with Neyo's new joint, *Crazy*, playing in the background. Monte wasn't as naïve as Brezell believed him to be, he knew exactly how to play his cards.

"Ain't nothing moving, the connect pulled back after the murders cause they suspected foul play and don't want no parts of that," Monte cautiously eye him.

"They won't deal with you?" Brezell asked, pretending to be needy.

"Naw, it's a done deal and besides, I got other plans," Monte stated firmly.

"What's that?" he asked in defense like, "yeah right".

"Komara and I are planning to move down to Houston or Dallas closer to your sister since she doesn't have plans on coming back with all that's happened lately."

"Really," Brezell said, playing stunned.

Brezell secretly despised Komara because he knew that she had been Monte's mistress when his mother was living. He felt like if he got revenge on everybody that ever hurt his mother, her spirit would officially be put to rest. Komara was one on the list. In his deranged mind, violating her would be more satisfying.

"Dag pops, you seem to have it all mapped out already," he stated with falsifying concern.

"I just know you will be okay out here. You're a survivor, a hustler, you'd sell snow in hell," he said patting Brezell's shoulder and boosting his ego. Before he said his next comment, Brezell could see he was studying his face to be sure to detect any change in expression after he spoke. "I've been meaning to tell you, the word is BG ain't gonna die. So, I went to visit him to find out if he could give up any details of the murders."

Being the master of deception and a great manipulator Brezell didn't change his expression at all.

"Yeah, that's good. I've been up there too," he lied. "The last time I was there dude was speechless."

"That's about an accurate description. He's still holding on as a veggie. You know his parents hired a private detective on his behalf," Monte confirmed.

"Word. They're going all out, huh?" Brezell remained together knowing it was eating the hell out of him that BG survived. With the update that BG's brain was damn near done, it helped him stay reserved. "Good for them. Let's order, I'm starved," he said, changing the subject.

Monte sat and observed Brezell's arrogance. Everything was playing in his favor, but to Monte, he knew his son setting himself up for destruction. Monte suspected his hatin' ass grimy son was behind John Otis's elimination, but he couldn't prove it. He knew this was coming since the day he witnessed his estranged wife's suicide and purposely left her diary for Brezell to read. In reality, Monte played out his plan to get out the game remaining hood rich, along with getting revenge on JO for cheating with his wife. Not only that, but possibly impregnating her Brezell. He knew the entire time that JO and Tina had been creeping for years. For JO to be his main man, it hurt. He would never do anything to hurt John Otis, yet JO always felt like he had to have the upper hand on everything and everybody. He could've had any female he wanted, but why his Tina? Monte loved her with all his heart, she was his high school sweet heart – his first love –the only female he knew for sure loved him genuinely.

The scandal...

Monte picked up on the dramatizing affair slowly, but surely. He suspected Tina's disloyalty, but never in a million years with his best friend. Tina used to leave the house, her whereabouts being unknown for hours at time. He knew signs of dishonorable actions because he strayed away himself at times. Monte thought that was all in part of being a man, but a woman should always stand her ground, play her position, and be that good, honest, faithful wife she signed up to be. To catch Tina, he started off by memorizing the color of panties she left the house in. Being raised by a single father, father and son conversations consisted of tutorials of how not to get caught cheating.

"Never wash your body with soap outside of the soap your woman buys. Always keep a fresh bar of the same soap in your car. You can always justify that, nigga. Never change your boxers, because whether you know it or not, your girl saw what pair you left the house in. Never allow the other chick to leave evidence, (make-up on your clothes, perfume smell, earrings left in the car, etc.). Bitches are slicker than you think, sly little ho's, but you gotta let them know, you can't out slick a pimp." The wise Mr. Wright used to coach him all the time.

One of Tina's biggest mistakes was she used to come home and get straight in the shower; a dead give away. When she got bold enough, she'd changed her panties before coming home. Monte played along, pretending to be ignorant to the entire ordeal. When, he already had phone conversations recorded, learning every detail. Distressed and heartbroken, he'd playback recording of Tina and JO deceiving him over the phone and many times, in his own house. What broke him down the most was to hear his wife brag to a mutual friend, in detail, about how she loved John Otis and longed to be with him. Monte knew this would never happen and instead of allowing the deceit to kill him, it only made him stronger. That's when he began to plot his way out. It wasn't until he stumbled upon Tina's diary that he learned secrets only she knew. He learned that JO and Tina had been creeping since they'd been together. He thought John Otis hooked them up as a good look for him, since he was already dating a dime, Kim. He also learned that Tina was uncertain about Brezell being his son and prayed that JO was the father. That's why she named his first name Jonathan and not Brezell because of how close she and JO were.

Just like the bitch on the side, things started going bad causing John Otis to lose interest in Tina when she pressured him to leave Kim and run off with her. Not being able to handle such rejection caused her to go into a deep depression and misery, holding tight to the secret of conceiving a child out of their affair. Things were getting so bad for her, living with this dark secret and her own treachery turning on her, she starting seeing a shrink. One day after returning from a therapy session, she walked into the house, startled by the radio blasting a conversation between two females. She heard her own voice along with the familiar voices of others she had spoken to over time and could remember sharing confidential information with over the phone. The surround sound was loud as she heard her own laughing and whispering to her confidants. She froze in fear, panicking while entering her bedroom only to find Monte patiently waiting on the bed with her dairy in his hand. He stared at her with disgust in his eyes. His expression alone made Tina's heart flutter.

"I can't ever trust you again. Bitch, you're a mothafuckin' enemy to me. People always say watch the ones closest to you, but you're my wife. How could you?" Monte boiled in fury.

"I, um, it, um, he, um." Tina couldn't find any words to justify his truth about her. There was nothing to say. No spoken words would describe the damage she had caused, so she took the defensive way out. "I'm sick, baby. All I can say is that I have an illness and the medication and the therapist are helping me get better," she cried with bucket teardrops, trying any routine to save her ass.

"I know yo ass don't think I'm that fuckin' dumb, do you?" he shouted, opening her dairy. "January 6, 1988. I hate being here with Monte, he ain't no made nigga. He ain't nothing, but JO's shadow. Now he's a real man. He fucks...'"

"Stop it!" Tina screamed, stopping him before he could finish mocking her diary.

"You weren't sick then, were you? That damn illness didn't stop you from sucking and fucking JO did it? Hell naw, so you and that fake ass syndrome can kiss my ass." He paced the floor to calm himself down. "You got me on this Jerry Springer type shit, got a nigga out here looking bad."

Monte had to punch the wall to stop from knocking Tina out. Tina just wept out loud; sobbing like somebody had just died.

"I hate you, Tina, and I want you out of my house by the end of this month. I'll stay somewhere else until you are out of here, but I'm telling you now, stay the fuck away from me," he said pointing viciously into Tina's forehead.

One good thing his father taught him was never, ever, under any circumstances, hit a woman.

"They are powerless to a raging man; don't ever do a woman like that. You wouldn't want it being done to your sister, mother, or daughter."

As bad as he wanted to grab Tina by the throat, he resisted.

"I can't, I can't be without you. Please, please, don't do this, Monte," Tina pleaded to her husband.

"What do you mean, 'don't do this'? No the fuck you didn't just say, 'don't do this.' You lucky I don't kill yo ass!" he shot back at her abruptly.

"I can't be without you. I don't know how to be without you. I'd kill myself if I couldn't be with you, I swear." Tina pleaded.

"Not me, I'm not that nigga. I'm his shadow, remember, so I guess now you two can live happily ever after. Oh no, wait," Monte paused to retrieve the diary and quote directly from her words, "February 10, 1988. I love John Otis. I just wish we could live happily ever after, but he barely speaks to my ass anymore. I feel like I can't live without him. My therapist said my thinking like that isn't helping my condition."

Monte stopped reading to gain his composure.

"That nigga, the one that got you going crazy and shit, he's the reason you deserve to die," he retorted.

Tina calmly started to undress, leaving Monte puzzled and confused. She got her a cup of water and her bottle of medication and got in the bed as if she was ready to go to sleep. He knew she was prescribed many pills to help with her Bipolar condition. After watching her pop at least 15 pills, he knew this wasn't normal, though. Out of resentment, he didn't try to stop her and he didn't call for help. He simply took it as a bluff, a way for her to get sympathy from him.

Tina didn't say another word. Life, as she knew it, was over in hours. She couldn't live without Monte and JO. They were her life support, the only loves she knew. Growing up in various foster homes with no family ties, she never had a job, didn't finish high school, and never had money of her own. She was totally dependent on being a hustler's wife. Everything was becoming a blur as she watched Monte fade out other life.

Monte didn't know if she could hear him or not, but he couldn't resist letting her know that regardless of her popping pills, it hadn't changed a thing.

"When you wake up, shit still gon' be the same. No pill can wash away you being a ho!" Monte shouted to his wife, placing her diary in her free hand. The other hand engaged with an empty pill bottle. He reclaimed the recorded tapes from the stereo system and left the house.

In an hour or so, he knew Brezell and Cashay would arrive home. If they arrived in time, it was a possibility she'd survive with medical attention. However, Cashay hadn't come home and Brezell came home hours later, too late to save his mother.

Nobody's fool

Months had passed and Monte and Komara were preparing for their big move to Houston, Texas with Cashay. Brezell was preparing for his big re-up in New York, along with Bionca and Chloe was contemplating how to tell her husband the big news; she'd just found out she was 12 weeks pregnant.

Life seemed to be going in everyone's favor except for BG's family. It had been over 11 months and the detective they hired, Detective Stark, had no leads except for the fact that BG's last incoming call was from Brezell's cell phone. When he questioned Brezell, he stated they were supposed to meet at the pool hall, but BG left before he showed up, which checked out to be true. Brezell had a solid alibi, but Detective Stark was determined to tie Brezell's shiesty ass to the crime in some type of way. His gut feeling told him Brezell was lying. Although, Detective Stark didn't know Brezell personally, just by brief conversation, he could read Brezell's body language.

Diary of a Kingpin's Daughter

Dear Diary,

They say when some one passes a new life is given. Be the first to know that I'm pregnant, about 12 weeks to be exact. I'm having mixed emotions. It's a blessing, but things are not right in my life for me to bring a baby in this world. I barely see Brezell anymore. I don't want to be a single mother. Maybe things will change when I tell him about the baby. Hopefully he will be as excited as I am about our first baby. Instead of cashing out on my parents home, I've decided to add money to the money they left me in my trust fund and have it put in my unborn child's name. I'm not hurting for anything and we have plenty of funds. Now I can assure that my child will be set for years to come.

This detective came over the other day asking all types of questions about daddy, Brezell, and BG. I told him I never knew of BG having any dealings whatsoever with daddy. He asked me what the connection was with BG and Brezell. That visit really scared me, especially since he was implying that Brezell might be knowledgeable about some info. I'm going to talk to Brezell about it, whenever I see him.

School started and I didn't even go register. I keep getting mail about losing my seat if I don't respond by the deadline. Truthfully, I don't even care. I have other things to worry about; the school thing will have to wait.

I can't believe I'm about to be a mommy. I hope it's a boy so I can honor daddy with his name.

It's ya girl,

Chloe Baguette Carter-Wright

Sideline Ho

Brezell came walking in the house at about 7am and he had the nerve to be crabby. Chloe was already up reading the Iyanla Vanzant guide to a happier and more spiritual life. Her sleep pattern was so messed up, she was bound to be up and occupied at any given time of day or night. Brezell came in and got straight in the bed. She decided to allow him to get some sleep while she cleaned the house and cooked breakfast. Brezell came down hours later in his boxers, still half-sleep, immediately picking with her.

"What the fuck are you burning?" he grumbled.

"Good morning to you, too," she said, sarcastically. "Are you hungry?"

"Naw, just pour me some apple juice," Brezell said blowing his nose. "Have you talked to your parent's lawyer, yet?" he questioned curtly.

That was the last thing Chloe wanted to discuss, she was ready to get the conversation going about the pregnancy; she was excited about the news. She had what felt like a billion questions to ask and a zillion things to tell him. He ruined the mood with his approach. She knew mentioning the detective's visit would agitate him even more, but she decided to go ahead and mention it anyway.

"Some detective came over here the other day," she stated plainly, handing him a glass of orange juice.

"What the hell you mean, 'some detective' who the fuck was it?" Brezell shouted short-tempered.

Chloe walked to the kitchen drawer and handed Brezell the card with the detective's information on it.

"Private Detective Waymon Stark." Brezell read slowly. "What did he want and what did you tell him?"

"He asked questions about the connection between BG, my dad, and you," she responded, almost trembling from the sound of his voice and the look in his eyes. Before she could finish telling him what was talked about, Brezell slapped her so hard that she fell to the floor.

"Bitch, you let some detective in my house, openly telling him what he wanted to know." He shouted standing over her. "Tell me exactly what you told him, word-for-fucking- word," Brezell demanded outraged.

"I only told him that JO barely knew BG and that you hung with him periodically, and you were at the pool hall when it all happened, that's it," she cried holding her stinging face.

"You stupid ass ho, why the fuck didn't you call me while that muthafucka was here?" Brezell's voice rose to a dangerous height. He continued to swing, as Chloe lay balled up in a fetal position trying to protect her stomach.

Once again, Brezell turned into this person she didn't recognize. He appeared deranged as he whaled at her uncontrollably.

"Please stop, stop, I'm pregnant," she managed to shout out in agony. Her face throbbed as automatic swelling set into her eye. Brezell took this plea as a bribe for him to stop the beating.

"Why are you lying to me? Look what you made me do; this is all your fault." Brezell rambled on and on as Chloe sat in the corner of the kitchen in fear of another attack. "What the fuck am I going to do? Fuck, fuck!" Brezell continued to rant and rave.

Chloe didn't know if he was referring to the detective or the pregnancy. She sat and cried silently, hoping not to draw his attention back to her. She flinched when he walked over to her.

"I just need to think, that's all, and it'll be okay. I'll make sure of that," Brezell said wiping some of the blood from her nose.

Again she did not know to which situation he was referring. She hesitantly accepted his embrace and his silent apology. She was in severe pain, with a possible sprained wrist, but out of complete fear, she remained silent. She knew that should have been a sign to get away from Brezell.

"Go clean ya'self up. Pop a pill and rest." He demanded her.

Instead of popping a pill, she cleaned herself up and took a little cat nap. When she woke up from her brief nap, she heard a funny noise coming from the bathroom adjoining their room. Her body was sore and achy from the maltreatment. She called out to Brezell, but received no response.

"Brezell?"

Sniff, sniff, cuk, sniff, cuk, cuk, Brezell devoured the last of the four white lines of cocaine with a dismantled pin, in a straw form, that lay before him on a glass plate. She stood frozen in surprise and disappointment. In fear of him seeing her, she got back in the bed and pretended to be asleep. She was embarrassed for him and feared another lash-out if he knew she peeked from the other side of the cracked door.

That's what his fuckin' problem is. He's a cokehead! She thought.

Seconds later, Brezell came out of the bathroom and back to the bed. Chloe prayed he did not pick up on her panicky spirit. She couldn't believe he was a victim to the very same drug he sold, a victim to the same state he often bashed. The first thing that came to her mind was the baby. She didn't know much about drugs, but she wasn't sure how much affect his addiction would have on their child. He nudged her in the back in attempts to wake her false sleep. She pretended to come out of a light sleep and focused her vision to his frame in front of her. Brezell's eyes appeared glossy and his movement was slow. His mood seemed more relaxed. She wanted so badly to let him know that she knew he tooted dope, but she was scared to death.

Instead of him talking, Brezell began to tug at her pajama shorts, signaling for her to take them off. Chloe nervously obeyed. Brezell rubbed his limp dick across her opening, attempting to get himself erect. Her body felt frozen and tense to his touch. His touch had become so unfamiliar to her; she had so much bitterness towards him now. This wasn't the man she fell in love with. This wasn't the same man that asked her father for her hand in marriage. This definitely wasn't the man she loved since she was 14-years-old. This man was a foreigner to her. His actions, his voice, his touch, his love wasn't the same.

After several unsuccessful attempts, Brezell fell into a quick sleep, snoring like he hadn't just attempted intercourse.

Chloe jumped from the bed and began to look through the pockets of his jeans and his jacket that lay openly across the ottoman at the end of the bed. Immediately, her hand met his vibrating phone at the first reach. The caller hung up and immediately redialed. Out of curiosity, she picked up the phone and listened.

"Hello, hello, Breezy!" the caller shouted anxiously. "Stop playing. On the real, I need you, your son is hurt!! Hello? Brezell?" the familiar voice shouted franticly.

Chloe's heart skipped a few beats and seemed to stop at least a second. Not only did she know the caller, but she wanted to know what the fuck she was calling Brezell about her baby for and claiming the child as Brezell's son. It just didn't add up to her at the time. She hung the phone up and placed it back in his jacket pocket. She felt the phone continue to vibrate as she placed the jacket back onto the ottoman. Her mind drew a blank; she didn't know what to think. She wanted answers, but was too afraid of the truth.

This couldn't be true, what did Brezell have to do with Bionca? Why was she calling his phone talking about 'your baby'?

Chloe didn't want to believe it; one of her former best friends had a baby with her husband. She eagerly wanted to know. She knew Brezell wasn't going to be of any assistance for the next couple of hours with him being in his deep sleep. She threw on a jogging suit and headed out the door.

Driving over to Bionca's house had Chloe's stomach in knots. She was so nervous. Not at all scared, but uneasy of what was left to find out and what Brezell would do once he found out her discovery. She knew B's character; she knew how Bianca got down. They once told each other everything. Once upon time, they shared secrets, clothes, and advice. Never in a million years could she imagine sharing her husband with a friend. She wished she had someone to comfort her. The distance between Cashay and Taylor's college ripped their bond. It was times like this that Chloe felt the need for a good friend by her side for support. She had become so secretive lately, wanting everyone to think she had the ideal life, rarely returned phone calls anymore. Her mind drifted to the good times she had with her high school friends. It saddened her to think they had come to this. She had no intentions to fight Bionca; she only wanted answers. She knew B well, she remembered how aggressive Bionca could be so she really didn't know what to expect. As she made the drive over to the projects, everything was starting to add up. Now Chloe realized why Bionca stopped coming around, why Brezell insisted she cut her off and leave their friendship past tense. There were many times she confided in Brezell how she missed Bionca so much and wanted to reestablish their friendship.

Now the truth was exposed, she was carrying Brezell's baby at her graduation and engagement party. Thinking all the way back to Cashay's graduation party when she noticed Bionca and Brezell were in each other's mix a little too much. Chloe thought of who else could've known about this private affair. She

Diary of a Kingpin's Daughter

wondered if Cashay knew of all her brother's evil, womanizing ways.

Why would he put me through this, why me, why now? She had to calm herself down feeling another break down coming on. The butterflies fluttered terribly in her stomach as she did 90 mph triumphing to Bionca's house to unveil what she hoped to be the accuracy of if all.

Knock, Knock, Knock! She could hear her heart beat to the rhythm of her bangs on Bionca's door. Chloe knocked for at least 5 minutes before one of the other Section 8 residents opened the door and stuck her prying face out.

"That girl left, she took that poor baby to the hospital. Stop beating on that door, chile," the women spoke through the small crack in her door. Before Chloe could ask any questions, she slammed the door shut. Chloe took a guess and drove to the county hospital in the hood not knowing for sure she would find Bionca there.

Chloe was going to the hospital with concern for Bionca's son more now than before. She was so confused. Her stomach cramped awfully as she speed-walked through the hospital. As soon as she hit the corner to where she was informed the room was, she saw Bionca standing at the pay phone sobbing to the person on the other end of the receiver. She just stared at Chloe with lament eyes.

"Chloe's here," Bionca stated to the listener on the other end of the phone. Chloe assumed the person asked what she was doing there just by Bionca's response, "Dunno, ask her. That's the last thing I'm worried about at this point, my son has 3rd degree burns, you really think I give a fuck about her right about now? You need to have your ass here and worry about that later, our baby is hurt!" she shouted through the receiver.

Right then, the sound of "our baby" stabbed Chloe mentality. She felt her tears streaming down her face. She was afraid to swallow in fear of choking off her own sorrow. Bionca hung up the phone and they faced each other, alone. Bionca had hate in her eyes mixed with the sadness from her son's state. Chloe couldn't think of anything she could have done to make this girl hate her as much as Bionca's expression was showing; to betray her as Bionca's actions had obviously shown.

"What the fuck do you want?" Bionca broke the silence.

"I'm not here to judge you. Is the baby okay?" Chloe asked wanting so badly to ask, How Bionca? Why? When? However, she decided to sympathize with her on her son's behalf and leave the questions for another time.

"Why do you care, you only came to ask about me and Brezell. I know you were the one who answered Brezell's phone and didn't say shit!"

"Yeah you're right, until I found out your son's condition, and then things changed." Chloe tried to assure her.

"Well, we don't need your pity so you can just leave. We are waiting on his daddy," Bionca said coldly, as if she had been waiting for the moment to throw that in her face.

"Bionca, you were my girl. What part of the game is this?" Chloe asked her trying to stop herself from howling a river.

"Bitch, please. You knew I was fucking Brezell in high school; act dumb if you want to, but you fuckin' knew. That same ignorance is what got you in with Brezell. You knew and pretended not to and you are still pretending. That's why I don't fuck wit yo fake ass. Yeah, I have Brezell's son and what you gone do? I'm not about to sit here and put in plain words what you already know. My child is hurt and I don't owe you shit, no explanation, no pity, not shit, so bounce before I make a scene."

Chloe felt like Bionca was challenging her. She stood frozen and speechless. This was not the time or place. She could no longer hold back her whales; she started to sigh out loud. Lately, crying seemed to be Chloe's only defense, but it left her so vulnerable.

"This is so messed up, Bionca, you know I didn't know. I suspected, but he denied it so I just left it alone. Why Bionca? That's real fucked up and you know it. Especially calling my phone and having your son call for his daddy when I pick up." Snot ran down her lip, she felt like she was four again; back when she fell off her bike after her father let the seat go allowing her to lose balance and hurt herself. She felt like John Otis had let her down by allowing her to injure herself. She felt like Brezell had done the same thing. He steered her wrong once again causing her to hurt and feel pain.

"Bitch, please. I never had my baby call your damn phone and I don't have to stand here and explain shit else to you. You better move around before I have security called on your weak ass! No, you know what... fuck you, Chloe! You always did think shit was a fairy tale, little Ms. Perfect. Don't ever step to me again in no type of way, ho. I'm not cha friend. I couldn't give a fuck less about you and it wasn't my baby calling. You might want to check Sheila, seeing as how she has a little Brezell as well." Bionca rolled her eyes and walked off.

She left Chloe standing there to sort out her own tribulations. Bionca always came off a little jealous of her in high school, but she never thought it was a love/hate friendship like that. Bionca must have had it out for her the entire time. Chloe stood there dumbfounded; she was lost in her own life. She began to think her entire relationship with Brezell was a swindle. Had she been an unwilling part of one big game? She remembered Sheila; she was the ghetto chick from the mall. Brezell had a lot of explaining to do; along with a lot of packing because Chloe wanted him to leave her alone; she wanted out of this charade of a marriage. Even she knew this was going to be one of the hardest tasks to follow. With Brezell's latest violent outbursts, things could get very messy.

Dear Diary,

My life has swirled out of control. I really think I've reached a point of insanity. I can't sleep and I barely eat. I've lost my will to live, my drive, and my self-worth. I've grown to resent my husband with every moving muscle in my body. I feel like the worlds against me, Lord. Brezell fathered two children outside of our marriage, one being with a past friend of mine. I plan to look into getting our marriage annulled. It was a deception from the beginning. I promise if it wasn't for my unborn child, I'd probably do something very vengeful to Brezell and Bionca. I wonder if Cashay knew of all of this. Honestly, I don't want to know, it would only be more hurt. I'm glad I never mentioned to Brezell that I'd met with my parent's lawyer. Of course they left me everything, so positive things will be lovely for me, without him. Truthfully better. I put a lot of it in an account for the baby, under "Baby Wright." Squeak's been asking me to move out of state with her, I'm really starting to consider it. I have so many unanswered questions that I know will be left in the air. This nigga stripped me of everything I've ever stood for. I hate his guts!!! No if, ands, or buts about it; I want out! That's final, no room for fraudulent apologies. I can't take anymore of this drama... this can't be life, this can't be love~

It's ya girl,

Chloe Baguette Carter-Wright

Jump off, jump off, ya girls a jump-off – their motives...

Sheila

At first, Sheila never thought it would work, applying for high school as an eighteen year old. There she was, 23, with a 7-year-old child. Do the math. She was 16 popping out a premature baby girl, 2 ½ months early. Shit, life is hard in the boogie down; at least it is for a child trying to raise herself. Life never did her any favors nothing short of hell on earth. At five, she was making her own dinner, washing her own clothes, combing her own hair, and sending herself off to school. By age 10, she was a full-time grown up and a full-time booster, making her own money to take care of herself. Believe it or not, her mom wasn't a dope fiend or nothing like that. True enough she was a single parent, but shit, she joined a number of women who were also. Her excuse was irresponsibility and pure old laziness along with the obsession to be loved by a man. Her favorite excuse was she took care of herself at an early age so now Sheila had to learn. The dumb bitch was just worthless and basically didn't give a damn about her daughter. All she needed to make her happy was some dick. Too bad the dick she fell in love with had the worst habit known to man, a heroin addiction.

She often talked down to Sheila, whose real name was Marquita, for no reason.

"Nasty little slut, ugly bitch."

Those were her favorite words to her when the world or her man was letting her down. She put any man that paid her attention before her daughter. The least Sheila could say about her so-called mother is she did buy groceries and pay the bills. She was grateful of that. Christmas never visited her and half the time, her mom forgot her birthday and other holidays. She could only remember her mom telling her she loved her one time in her entire life. One of her niggas went upside her head and took her welfare check. They hid in the closet while he and one of his crack head friends got high in their kitchen. She held Sheila's head close to her chest and she whispered, "We're all we got, each other, I love you, baby."

At that moment, Sheila felt loved and nothing else mattered. Well guess what, when that nigga's high went down, she was put on the back burner as usual. Sheila never knew her father and her mom burned so many bridges with her family members, nobody in the fam really fucked with them.

Sheila just had to go and grow her some full-sized breasts and a shapely ass, didn't she? That would make it sweet.

You got to use what you got to get what you want. A bitch with a pussy should never be broke. Is what Sheila was taught.

It was then she started searching for something or somebody to love her. She desperately wanted to know what it was her momma loved so much about a man and you better believe her little hot ass went looking. At thirteen, she wasn't boosting out of kid stores; she went straight to the grown-up department stores. She wore everything from miniskirts to see-through shirts. It was a wonder she didn't get pregnant until she was 15½, especially since she lost her virginity at twelve. She started off fucking little boys in middle school, whenever she did decide to go. Then she moved onto the small-time hustlers on the block. They used her little body so much that it allowed her to graduate to the big leagues by the time she was 16. She got knocked up by a nickel and dimmer named Thomas, who got busted two weeks after Nautica Simone aka "Na-Na", their baby girl, was born. Most complain about the affects a baby has on the body. Shit, not Sheila, she was ready to congratulate it. That baby helped her form even wider hips, a fatter ass, and fuller breasts.

That's when she met Julius aka "Ju-Ju", a 26-year-old, accomplished neighborhood dope boy. Now at 16, Sheila had the body of a 25-year-old. She thought she was ready for the big leagues, fucking with Ju-Ju. She thought she had hit the jackpot. That nigga whipped her young ass and had her thinking she was in love. He nurtured her young mind with sex, lies, and money. She was willing to do pretty much whatever he asked. His wish was her command. The nigga had her transporting work, using people's social security numbers to come up on credit cards, phones, and whatever else credit could buy without the exchange for money. She even did instant credits in all the department stores in her name and whoever else's name that got caught slipping with their identity. He took care of her and she repaid him with her body and her various hustles. Fucking around with Julius is how she ended up in Chicago, registering for high school in somebody else's name, living someone else's name. When Julius got indicted, the feds came for her. His drug fam knew how involved Sheila was with his hustle and how much info she had on him and they feared further charges being brought on him and his posse if she was to snitch. So his cousin, Seven, arranged a new life for her in Chicago under a bogus name of some loser ass chick that allowed her individuality to be bought for some chump change. Since she had dropped out of high school, it was easy for Sheila to transfer her transcripts to another state. Only thing she had to do was stay out of school and out of the morgue. Everything else fell into place.

The loser bitch, Sheila Jones, didn't do shit but smoke weed all day and fuck the locals all night. Seven made sure she had a nonstop supply of hydro and pocket money, as long as she never blew her cover. She didn't have a record and her credit was already shot so she was pretty much a waste of skin. Picking up as her in another state wasn't hard. She left her daughter, Nautica, with one of her home girls that she trusted would take care of her, Tanya. Tanya already had a daughter Na-Na's age so she knew Tanya would do right by her. Tanya pretended to be her sister by the father they never met so the county gave her assistance and declared Nautica abandoned by her parents. Her deadbeat ass daddy signed over his rights so as far as her baby was concerned she was straight.

Seven picked Chicago because that's where he was originally from. He moved to New York when he was 17 and never came back. He helped Sheila set up her apartment and made sure she got in school then; he bounced but still had frequent visits to hold her down. She didn't want to spend the rest of her young years behind bars pumping pussies with no other ho so she was all game for her big move. It wasn't hard signing herself up for school, especially since she had all the needed paper work and she was supposedly turning 18 in a few months. She was declared a senior at Thornton High School. She knew she wasn't going to go get no job so school didn't sound so bad. She had to do something to waste time and meet me a young fool. That's where she met Brezell. She never was the type to hang with females so she was a loner from day one. Seven left her a nice little ride and a stash, which he refilled monthly and she was set. Brezell and Sheila were in the same homeroom and they had lunch hour together. From the first time she saw his sexy black ass, she knew she had to have him. One day at lunch, she invited him over after school. She was really enjoying reliving her teenage years.

"Is your mother going to be there?" he asked before accepting her invite.

"Hell naw, I stay by myself. I'm a grown ass woman," she replied almost forgetting to stick to the script.

"From the looks of it, I can tell," Brezell said, undressing her with his eyes. Sheila fucked the shit out of him the first day he came by and had been addicted ever since. He claimed he didn't like people in his business so they never let it be known that they messed around at school. That was cool with her; she barely associated with anybody anyway. She started hanging out with her neighbor, Brea, on a regular basis. Brea was amazed at the 18-year-old PYT making it on her own in the windy city. She gave Sheila the run down on Brezell and his affiliates, including other hood legends. Brea was 21, no kids, and living in low-income housing. Sheila liked her from jump;

she seemed bonafide. The only thing she didn't like about her was she was too materialistic and thought she had to be up on everything. The latest fashion, styles, nigga's, gossip, cars, whatever it was, she thought she was the connoisseur.

She wanted to be the first to know so she could be like, "Ah, they got that from me." She was a cute chick though. She had smooth, light-brown skin and she wore her hair blonde at the top with dark brown at the bottom. She kept her hair in roller wraps with full pretty curls. She appeared to be high-maintenance, but her ass was struggling to pay the rent just like the rest of the hood bitches. She fucked with John Otis, off and on, on the down low, but who didn't? JO practically gave dick away. She said she had been fucking that nigga since she was 16. That's how Sheila got the inside on everything and knew Brezell had potential to be that nigga. That's why she hand-picked Brezell to do business with Seven in New York. She dug his hustle and saw baller potential written all over him. Since most of time males make it further in the dope game than females, Sheila just knew Brezell would take this shit on headfirst. He was indeed a leader and far from a follower.

Most girls grow up wanting to marry and have children by professional athletes, lawyers, doctors, and whatnot. Shiiit! Sheila always dreamt of being the main bitch of the wealthiest baller. Why not? You get all the same perks and much more respect. If you don't end up abused or, in a bodybag, but those were the risks you took. It wasn't even about the money; she wasn't hurting for any money. Shit, she was a hustling bitch herself. She could sell fire to the devil; it was just something about the feeling she got being around a real ass, hood rich ass, thugged out ass nigga. It gave her an unexplainable rush. She watched Brezell get off hundred dollar sacks for almost a year before she offered him a promotion. Seven was trying to step out his region and make more moves, Brezell was eligible so she referred him and the rest is history. He received, of course, and she just knew this would earn her first dibs on being a hustler's main chick. Brezell used to come lay up at her house all the time in the beginning. She even gave that nigga a key to her crib. She never told him her secret of her real age and identity, but he could tell from the way she sucked him off that she was a well-experienced certified head doctor. She planned to play her cards right this time around. It was like she had a second chance to relive life and do things differently; hopefully to her advantage this time. And just like the first time, she had to catch feelings and end up pregnant by another dog ass nigga. Brezell had no idea she already had a shorty. He didn't have any kids yet, so when Sheila told him she was pregnant with his son, he was overjoyed. Nigga got to buying all types of shit. He didn't stay captivated too long though.

Some bullshit had to be thrown in the game. Sheila was so jealous that Brezell had Chloe tatted on his neck so she fucked off with Dean, another ghetto celebrity and it got back. She put in too much work. She grinned with this nigga damn near two years, took plenty penitentiary chances, and this fool ass nigga turned around and married Chloe's pathetic ass. That's why she began sexing and was unsure who her son's father was.

Brezell had some serious control issues going on. He expected Sheila to just sit back while he and that ho played house and make herself available to his convenience. She didn't think so. She was not that bitch! One time, Brezell came over and Dean was there, Brezell shot Sheila a look of venom and she automatically knew not to play any games. She had to dismiss Dean before she got them both killed. Brezell put his hands on her that night. She saw a side of him that wasn't for any shit and even though she was left bruised and broken up, she actually thought that meant he cared. She felt like she had him in his chest to show that much emotion. She just knew that nigga had caught feelings, too. Ever since, Sheila just accepted the fact that she was #2 and waited on her turn to have him. A monkey wrench was thrown in her game when this other chick – Bionca, went and got knocked up by his loose dick right after she did. But he still did his part with Sheila and her son, but she wanted him, not his support. It was just something about that nigga that had her obsessed. She's a hood bitch and she liked hood shit so maybe it was the way all those tats looked reflecting off his sweaty, black skin after hours of fucking or maybe it was his belligerence. She loved the way that thick vain popped out the side of his neck when he got mad or overexcited. She especially loved a man that gambled and smoked weed. She just loved his gangsta. Not to mention, he reminded her of one of the dope boys from back home with his baggy jeans and Timbos.

Whatever the case may be, Breezy had her going through it. She had it bad. She used to call and play on Chloe's phone. She had lil' Brezell calling for his daddy or just baby talk through the phone. He thought it was all fun and games, but really his momma was trying to drive the broad crazy. She just hoped Chloe would never get her number changed. Once, she egged the bitch's car. She knew about his other ho on the side, Bionca, and a few other trivial females, but she wasn't tripping on them. Their status wasn't any better than hers with the nigga and she knew damn well he didn't give a fuck about the Bionca chick. He made that whore a prospect, too. She wasn't a threat, Chloe was and Sheila was determined one way or another to run the prissy little bird off, knock her out the box. Then she knew for sure that she would be next in line to be wifey. She considered herself a down bitch. She put her man on and she was willing to ride or die. It didn't bother her that he went upside her head every now and again. A bitch like her needed to be checked real well every now and then because she was one to test a nigga. She could put some words together, make a nigga wanna leave forever until she lay that head game down. It's nothing though. A bitch was patient. She was just going to wait her turn, but one thing for certain and two things for sure, she was determined to get rid of Chloe, one way or another.

Brea

"Life is a bitch and then you die." That was Brea's mother's way of explaining why she stayed in an unhappy relationship for over 19 years. Her mom and dad got married straight out of high school because she was pregnant with Bre. Back in their day, that was the thing to do. Brea grew up in a big, pretty house with a white picket fence with a dog. From the outside looking in, life was perfect, but once you walked through the door into this perfect house, things weren't as ideal as they appeared. She lived in a house where her parents didn't sleep in the same room and words were hardly exchanged between the two. It was strange because in public, they put on their happy faces and they performed to be one big happy family, Brea, her daddy, their dog, Louie V, and her mom.

Just like an unwritten law, Brea knew not to talk about it. Not to mention constant reminders from both of her parents not to discuss with outsiders about what went on in their home. Her relationship with her mom was very strained, but she and her dad kept their bond. They used to go skating every Sunday until her daddy found comfort in the arms of various women, and then his little girl wasn't as important anymore. Without her dad, skating every Sunday afternoon turned into skating every Sunday night where it was known to be that spot to get it in.

That's when she met John Otis. All the popular moneymakers, hustler groupies, and real skaters went to the rink on Sunday nights. She heard about the jump off through her 20 year old cousin, Kia. Kia went for one purpose only, to hook up with ballers and thought she got lucky when JO appeared one night to drop Chloe off. She put on her best picked outfit for the day, her smell goods, and flaunted her ass around the rink, gaining everybody's attention except JO's. Kia begged 16 year old Brea to approach him for her and unafraid, she agreed. Brea tried to hook her up, but JO wasn't interested in her cousin.

Instead of him inquiring about Kia, he pushed up on her.

"What's up with you youngin'?" he asked Brea.

Brea knew he liked young girls because she used to hear this other young bitch named Karma brag about what he did for her, so Brea knew he was paid and very generous. She felt bad for Kia, but she also felt like there was no need in letting him go to waste; one of them had to have him and he picked her.

She told JO she was eighteen at first until he asked her to get a hotel room in her name and then she had to tell him the truth. He still didn't care. When she finally did turn eighteen, she was still continuously sexing him. They grew to be very close and she considered him her sugar daddy. Ms. Jonesy, the gossip radio reporter didn't have shit on their pillow talk.

John Otis told young Brea things about his affairs with women and even bragged about banging his closets friend's wife. He told her, in detail, how Tina got emotionally attached and wanted to make sure she stayed in check. He even told her that he thought the son, that he called his godson, Tina had was possibly his until he found out he wasn't when he secretly took him to get a DNA test.

Brea knew JO wasn't worth much to her for very long. He tricked off too much and she didn't like the way he yapped off. She intended to get it while the getting was good. She looked at the situation like this, *If a nigga already got a main bitch and you are one of the few bitches he fucks with, the likelihood is, you're temporary. Niggas will fuck wit' you until his interest dies out, then it's on to the next bitch.* And Brea was not your average dumb young girl. She made future plans.

John Otis always taught her quality.

"Don't ever fuck with a nigga that pops major shit and broke as hell. If the nigga don't have his own crib, his own car and bitches flocking around him, chances are, that nigga broke and he only a nickel and dime, flunky ass nigga."

Brea knew not to wait around until he lost interest in her, so she made the first move. Just so happened her new prey was the godson,

Brezell. She didn't give a fuck though; she didn't have anything to do with those family secrets. Shit, it was like she never knew. She observed Brezell and carefully plotted out her next move. She sat back and watched as this young bitch, Sheila, groomed him into a boss. In fact, she admired her style.

Brea made friends with Sheila the minute she moved in so by the time she got the scoop on Brezell, Brea and Sheila were well-aquatinted and sharing secrets. Never once remembering a true bitches rule, if it's one thing you never do, is tell the next bitch how your man fucking you and how he's coming out his pocket. Sheila used to give detail by detail how her guy laid the pipe and how he was breaking bread. She didn't do nothing but build interest up until Brea rode his dick. Personally, Brea thought the bitch talked too much anyway. She used to tell her how dude was coming up and next in line to be H.N.I.C. The thought of him fucking Brea, her headboard hitting the wall that separated her room from Sheila's apartment made her adrenaline rush. First chance she got, that nigga was hitting her punanny and Sheila thought her head game was tight. Brea was confident about hers, JO taught her well and she studied the video technique of ole girl, Karrine Steffans, blow-for-blow. Wasn't nothing and nobody gonna stop Brea's operation.

▶ ▶ ▶ ▶ ▶

Brezell held Brea by her hair as he assured every last inch of his dick penetrated inside of her.

"Ahhh, Brezell, I need this dick, I'm lovin' it," Brea panted out between strokes.

"Whose pussy is this?" he asked, increasing his strokes.

"Yours, baby, all yours," Brea said as she struggled to loosen his grip on her hair.

He grabbed her by the neck, still stroking, "You still fucking JO? I know you are," he said replacing his look of pleasure with resentment.

"I promise I'm not, only you can hit this," Brea told him assuring him she was all his, especially since after months and months of convincing, he finally agreed to allow her to get insurance policies on the both of them. He thought it was smart of her to think of that, especially since his line of work was so dangerous and unpredictable. She was glad she got him to agree before he got married. She honestly did start to catch feelings for his dog ass. He was around enough that she never had to get jealous of Chloe, Bionca, or Sheila because, in her own strange way, she felt equal to all of them.

Brezell and Brea had grown so close; he didn't hide anything from her. She was so laid back and cool; a nigga couldn't help but get comfy with her. He did things for her and with her that she knew for a fact he didn't do for Sheila because if he did, she would have told her. He used to treat her to shopping sprees, mostly without him. The only rule was Brea had to buy two of everything; one for her and one for Chloe, which she didn't have a problem with as long as it came in more than one color or style. Some call it crazy, but she called it compromising.

Once, Sheila caught Brezell coming out of Brea's apartment. He told her he stopped by to handle some business with John Otis. Little did she know, Brea had stopped talking to JO a little after her son, Brezell, was born and he was going on three by this time. She could keep letting that nigga fool her into thinking Brea hustled with him and she fucked with his superior. She knew as well as Brea did, Brezell was a made man. Her ass doubled his status by plugging him with her people in New York. If she had paid attention to anything they ever talked about, it should have been a known fact that Brea, too, wanted to be the main bitch of a chief. The difference between Brea and Sheila was that Brea would rather be the beneficiary any day. She'd be damned if she were left broke with nothing but stories to tell about how she used to have her way out here. No, not Brea. She knew a few major points about fucking with a dope boy. They either ended up dead, in jail, or broke. So her best bet was to learn how to stash and plan for the day when it all came to an end.

Karma

Karma came into this world enclosed in the blood of a professional gold digger so it was certain that she would carry on the legacy strong as ever. That's why her mother named her Karma; Karma Allen Smith, to be exact. She claimed she had a long list of people to seek vengeance on; where she left off, she would prepare her daughter to continue her bequest. Karma's father, Allen "Alley Cat" Smith, never claimed her, so fuck him, too; she never claimed his ass either. He was supposedly another big shot in Chicago that lost the last of his good years to the system when he was indicted and now serving Federal time in prison. The nigga still had at least ten strong ones to go so he was no use to Karma any damn way. And the fact is she vaguely remembered him. She ran across some little bitch they called the Stiletto princess named, Modesty, a few times, which is his other daughter, the one he cared for, she assumed. That ho had the nerve to turn her nose up at her when they were introduced to each other as sisters. She was acting all high and mighty. Karma started to jap out on her crab ass, but was advised otherwise. Out of respect for her bloodline, she let it ride. They looked one and the same, but fuck her, too. And she snide her, "Bitch, don't let these stilettos fool you!"

Komara, her mother, raised her more like a little sister rather than a daughter. Naw, she wouldn't even say that much, it was more like she was her young protégée. From the day she could comprehend words, Komara taught Karma the ups, downs, ins, and outs of snagging, keeping, and breaking a wealthy man. The first rule of her on-going lesson was to never refer to her as mother, mom, mommy, and sure in the hell not momma. Komara was one of the strongest women she'd ever met. She admired her hustler's ambition; got to get it by any means necessary. When her moms put them out, she was 15, Karma was 2 years old, and Komara was still able to hold them down. She took many chances with various drug lords before she finally landed a lasting spot in the heart of Monte Wright. Yeah, he was the shadow to JO, but he was a mothafuckin' paid shadow.

Money Green and Komara were lovers for years, but were discreet about it because of his marriage and all. His only wish was for her to keep their affair top secret and in return, she would be taken care of. The situation turned into an unbreakable existence, that nigga raised her into a top of the feline line; her stock went up at least 50%. Komara never complained because Monte made sure she was fulfilled at all times. He put them up in a fat ass crib with a fly ass whip, a CLK Benz coupe to be specific, and he kept her account stacked as well. This is how

Karma met JO. The man practically watched her sprout into a mini version of Komara. By the time she hit her teen years, she was a beautiful young woman. She kept my hair short and colored at all times to compliment her small head and golden complexion. JO used to come over to their house with Monte all the time, sometimes with a female friend or two and at times, he came alone. The days he came solo were the days she looked forward to. She was only thirteen when the flirting started.

He would often tell her, "Damn, you're going to be a fine ass woman when you get older. I hope I still got my swagger when you reach 18."

"I'm already grown!" she would openly flirt back.

"No, little miss, you're still ripening. I have patience, I can wait." He would tease. When she told Komara of their minute dealings, she was ecstatic. She said JO was in the major leagues; she said Karma needed more grooming for him. But, she was happy he took notice because hooking him would be an automatic upgrade for her.

For three years, John Otis watched Karma mature into a full-grown lady. Although she was short, she filled out in all the right places. At 16, she was already doing what most young women don't do until they're into their early 20's. Komara assured Karma that she trained her well in the sex department, her favorite line was "power of the pussy", and her sex game was surely on point. No longer a virgin, Karma courted many money makers. It wasn't until she started going to the highly popular Sunday's at the skating rink, Harlem Nights, that John Otis broke his own pact. He could no longer hold back his lust for her perfectly shaped round ass and her supple B-cup breasts. She was only a freshman in high school, but was already ready for the senior of the streets. Her sweet sixteen couldn't have been any sweeter. John Otis bought Karma her first ride. She got a candy apple red Lexus coupe with "My Karma" on the plates. She was overwhelmed with that gift because she didn't expect it, plus his only child, Chloe, was still being car-pooled. The list of offerings she received was endless. Once, when she thought her well was running dry, Komara taught her how to soak it back up. She started being purposely seen with other elite hustlers to make JO jealous. After that, JO continuously stepped his game up in order to keep her to himself.

Komara always taught Karma, "Don't ever let him think he's the only one. You are young and tender make that old-man sweat. He's dying to keep that tight pussy."

Karma felt a little bad when Chloe befriended her. The feeling didn't last long because, as Komara always confirmed, it's all about survival of the fittest. Karma's being kept by JO was far more valuable to her than their caddy little friendship so with that known fact, she kept it moving.

John Otis wasn't just a provider to her; he was also a mentor. She admired him and held him in very high regard. He was such a wise man all the way around the board. Conversing with him was a tutorial every time. He was money smart, street smart, and a very worldly and knowledgeable man. He taught her how to save and invest.

"Got to have a stash to run to when the rain comes." He often coached. *"Keep the kitty stacked and full in case of emergency,"* he advised.

He often asked Karma what she wanted to do with herself. He wanted to make sure she had something to fall back on and also gain her own sense of independence. She didn't have any skills or special talents except the way she could twist those legs whatever direction he wanted them to go in. Other than that, she enjoyed doing hair and nails here and there.

Komara counseled her on how to get him to buy her a hair shop, so that they would have long money with, or, without JO. And that she did, JO fronted the money and Split Endz came to life.

At times, Komara seemed a tad bit envious. Her protégée was getting ahead of her and in all the years of her bopping from man to man, she was always left with material goods, nothing of substance like Karma's hair shop, which was doing extremely well. In the beginning, she was all game with Karma snagging John Otis, but after awhile she advised her otherwise.

At the last minute, she informed Karma that JO was her father's young advisee. Allen had started calling from jail when he got wind that his little girl was putting out to that grown ass man. Didn't mean a damn thing to Karma. However, when JO was unexpectedly murdered she knew she had to move forth – forth to the next best man – Brezell.

Diary of a Kingpin's Daughter

Dear Diary,

I feel so sick to my stomach right now. Since I've been getting myself together and keeping my ear to the street, I hear rumors that Brezell is creepin' off with this ho, that bitch. And the sad part about it these are all females that I know and that know me very well! Either way I feel betrayed. Most of all, I'm embarrassed. Everytime I look at one of these bitches, it's a reminder that they've had half of me. When I think of how he makes love to me, my stomach turns because I'm wondering if they get the same treatment. I never cheated on my husband, never thought about it. Here I am giving this negro the best of me and in return he's sharing his love. It's killing me 'cause I know these broads are sitting up laughing at me. I'm probably the talk of the nail shop. I feel so damn stupid. I'm Mrs. Faithful and almost every hoodrat on the block can say they had my man! That's not what I want nor, is it what I signed up for. I'm supposed to be special. I'm supposed to be his wife. I can't live with the fact that I'm sharing what's supposed to be mines!

I can't build up the courage to confront him because the last thing I want is confrontation, besides, he's gonna deny it anyway. And, probably back-ass hand my ass. Sometimes I wonder if it's me. Am I doing something wrong?

Am I not fulfilling my role as wifey? Maybe I can do better and it will keep my man from roaming?

Plus, I keep hearing that daddy was boning all these young girls, fucking off on my mom! Mostly, the same girls that Brezell is screwing. And I hope to God it's not true about daddy and Mrs. Tina.

It's ya gurl,
Chloe Baguette Carter-Wright

How sweet it was

Chloe woke up to hard blows to her face and body, unable to focus. She couldn't figure out what was going on other than somebody was pounding her fiercely.

"Bitch, I'ma give you something to ask about!" Brezell shouted while attacking her as if she could match his battle.

The last time she'd seen him was before she left in pursuit of Bionca, which was almost a week ago. She called Bionca's house a few times, but she called her number. She spent three days trying to find out exactly who Sheila was and where she could find her. Nobody was willing to help. She used to have the entire community to look out for her just on the strength of being John Otis' daughter. Since Brezell was in charge, things were different and a lot more complex. Brezell was a gorilla boss, it's like people ran under him out of fear and not to mention he was the hand that fed the hood now. At least when JO ran things, he was reasonable. Chloe didn't have anybody, her own family had turned their back on her in order to continue to receive a piece to eat, even Aunt Ryan. She was always a money hungry, greedy bitch anyway. The only person she had in her corner was Squeak and she was over 200 miles away back in St. Louis, continuing her service duty.

"I'm a grown ass man; you don't question shit I do!" He shouted while kicking Chloe like he lost his mind.

He had turned into this demon again.

"Call for your daddy now, bitch. Where's your hero? Call him now!" he said in rage.

The pain shot directly to her stomach, it out-weighed the damage he was doing to her body. Her legs became warm as the color of her pajama pants changed color instantly. Brezell calmed his rage in observance.

"What the fuck!" he said frantically.

"You're killing our baby!" Chloe cried out in pain.

Brezell look stunned as if her pregnancy was a surprise to him and then, picked her up and carried her to the tub.

"I need to go to the hospital; I could be having a miscarriage," she cringed out in pain. Chloe caught a glimpse of herself passing the mirror before he sat her down to undress her. Her lips were swollen and the blue and purple coloring was starting to appear on her right eye. Her entire body ached as her head throbbed at the same pace as her racing pulse.

"Naw, you'll be alright, you just need to soak, and I probably just scared the baby," he said suddenly sounding gentle and handling her more delicately. "Baby, I'm sorry, you hear me. I didn't mean to do this. I lost it. I am so sorry!" he said holding Chloe in his arms. "I wasn't thinking,

I'm high and I was scared. I swear I didn't mean it and had no idea you were carrying my baby!" he said pushing his crocodile tears out purposely.

It must've been the constant overuse of drugs causing him to have such a short-term recollection of her pregnancy. Brezell held Chloe's face in his hands, crying silently. She couldn't believe her current situation. As she sat in tub, the bath water turned light pink from the mixture of water and blood, her cramps slowly mellowed and the blood eased. Brezell pampered her until he felt her tense body calm. She never once looked up at him. She was so angry and ashamed. She was petrified of her own husband.

"I don't know what Bionca told you, but I'm letting you know right now, that's not my baby. Me and all the homies ran a train on her, she don't know who her baby daddy is. To keep it real with you, she even fucked JO," he said to save his own ass.

"Why I have to find out like this?" she asked with her head down, feeling defeated.

"I was going to tell you, I was just scared. I didn't want you to leave me. All I know is shorty ain't mine and I don't fuck with the bitch so I felt no need to talk about it. I was leaving that in the past and starting my life with you. You're who I love; you're the one I'm in love with. I got your name tatted all over my body." Brezell pleaded, trying hard to continue producing his obviously fake tears.

Chloe's heart felt heavy as she considered mercy. Brezell was like kryptonite to her soul, she felt like she had no power to resist him. She couldn't concentrate with the thought of a possible miscarriage haunting her mind.

"What about the baby?" she asked, in a kind way wanting permission to go to the hospital.

"What about him?" he quizzed, unsure of which baby she was referring to.

"Not Bionca's son. The baby I'm carrying. I think I'm having a miscarriage," Chloe mumbled.

"Ahh, you still bleeding?"

"No," she whined.

"Still in pain?" Brezell questioned.

"No, but, I..."

Brezell put his finger to her mouth to hush her. "You'll be okay, I'm here. I won't let anything happen to you. If we see more blood, then I'll take you, okay? I promise, its okay," he said apologetically.

She wasn't convinced, more frightened than anything, but being totally demoralized by him, she agreed.

Brezell didn't want her to be questioned about her bruised face and body at the hospital. No need for further investigation so he wanted to keep her home.

Dear Diary,

Brezell snapped out on me the other day; beat me like a fiend that tried to run off with a sack. I thought I lost the baby because I started bleeding. He finally allowed me to go the doctor four days later. The doctor said the baby was okay and stress caused the bleeding. They checked the baby's heart beat and it was okay. I wanted to get an ultrasound, but they wouldn't let me. I saw my doctor observing the fading bruises on my body; I read the concern in her eyes. I'm sure if Brezell wasn't present, she would have asked about them. I was thinking about leaving him for good – escaping this bitch – but I can't live in fear, not knowing when or what will cause Brezell's to snap. I guess fear is what's causing me to stay. Where would I go anyway? The first place he would check is St. Louis. I didn't tell anybody about my drama, yet. I'm hesitant to tell Squeak' cause I know she would jap out and I don't want her in the middle of my drama. Plus, I couldn't live with myself if something happened to my cousin because of me.

I didn't even bother to ask Brezell about Sheila. Brezell would deny it to the fullest anyway. A part of me wants to know the truth and the other half just wants to ignore it and go on living my life like it was before all this drama.

I'm just gonna play it cool for the safety of my baby and me. But for real, if he freaks out like that again, I'm just gone leave. I just hope it don't have to come to all that. I'll be okay; I know he felt bad about what happened. I could tell he was sorry; he's been extra nice and pampering me ever since. I know Brezell loves me, I just need to stop looking for shit to be mad at and stop making him upset.

It's ya girl,
Chloe Baguette Carter-Wright

New York, New York...

"The bitch Marquita done went up North and set up shop," Seven said puffing his joint.

"Oh yeah?" Mike said, wanting to know more. "I thought she was fighting a case?" he questioned.

"Naw, she was outta here before those peoples got to her," Seven said passing the marijuana. "I've always liked her cause she got the soul of a hustler and the spirit of a nigga. She knows how to get money more than half these bum ass scabs out here and she keeps the shit gully," Seven said rubbing his chin and grinning at the thought of Marquita Coleman, now known as Sheila Jones. "Yeah, the crab hooked up with some up north cat and the nigga made his way, now they up there getting it up 'big willie' style."

"Word!" Mike said, curious for more figures.

"Yeah, you remember that Arabian-looking dude Quita introduced us to when we stopped through? That cat; his ass started making double trips out here and shit got so good, he driving out now instead of flying and he stay bringing a bad piece with him. I wonder if that dude be fucking all those dames?" Seven asked.

"Aww, I remember seeing that mark when we made that trip to Chi-town. That one lil sack chaser, Brea, put me up on son," Mike said picturing Brezell in his head. "Is that nigga fucking with hay, too?" he asked, wanting a piece of the pie.

"Dunno, I'll ask. He a real live nigga, too. Word up, Ock. He ain't no sucka ass nigga so keep that shit gully with B and I'll put in a good word. Dude my peoples so don't do him dirty," Seven said grunting from the weed smoke caught in the passage of his chest and throat. He knew what type of foul shit Mike was usually on so he let him know to keep that shit to himself. Mike smiled at the possibility of a come up. Brezell was due in New York in less than a week.

To make things work smoothly, Brezell came home every night for almost two weeks to make sure Chloe was satisfied and to make up for putting his hands on her *again*. He demanded she get her cell phone number changed. He also planned to pop either Bionca or Shelia in the mouth. She claimed the anonymous baby called again saying, "Da-ddy, hi da-dddy," with a bitch giggling and snickering in the background. Brezell swore, if one of them bitches ruined his final plans with wifey, he would cancel their ass, too.

"Baby, I gotta run to NY tonight. Gotta handle some business. Go shopping; go get your hair done, or something. I'll be back in a few days," Brezell said preparing to leave. "I see you picking up some weight; I'm going to have me a pretty, little fat baby," he said rubbing Chloe's stomach. "Have you thought of a name, yet?" he questioned.

She got excited since this was his first time inquiring about the baby.

"Nakima Jocelle Carter-Wright," she said, proudly.

"I don't like that name," he said killing her joy.

"Why not? Nakima is from my mom's name and Jocelle is for JO, like daddy's." She hesitantly replied back. She had become so apprehensive around him.

"How do you know it's a girl and where is my name in it?" he asked, deliberately picking with her.

"I'll think of something else," she replied, saddened.

Brezell wanted to start a fight so he could remain gone from home longer with his new mistress, Karma. He was really feeling himself. He ran shit, both at home and in the streets. He was fucking everything moving, especially the ones he knew John Otis had dealt with in the past. He probably was taking his vendetta too far, but didn't really give a shit. Brezell's fling with Karma started when she agreed to allow him to have drugs shipped to her beauty salon as hair supplies. He didn't give a fuck about her ties to his wife and neither did she. Karma didn't see anything but green flashing in front of her eyes, she too couldn't care less about the phony friendship she maintained with Chloe. It was something about his swagg that all the women were drawn to.

"When I get back from the city, I want you to have thought about a new name for my baby girl," Brezell said, kissing Chloe on the forehead and heading for the door. Oddly, he always found delight in crushing her spirits. "And, ey bay, if you're a weak bitch, you'll get ran right over. You better get ya swag back, ma."

With that he left and he and Karma were in route to NY.

▶ ▶ ▶ ▶ ▶

Karma and Brezell arrived in New York as planned, after an 18-hour drive. Unbeknownst to them, they had been followed, as Brezell had been for months without knowledge. Detective Wymon Stark was determined to solve the attempted murder of his employer's son, Todd "BG" Wedderburn. They wanted the murder solved. More importantly, they wanted to find the monster that permanently disabled BG.

Brezell handled his business with Seven immediately and still had a few days to spare. Since Karma had never been to New York, they decided to tour the city and shop, hitting up all the trendy spots. They even hit up a club; a fashionable spot called 40/40, which was the brainchild of rapper, turned business mogul and CEO, Jay-Z.

While at the club, Brezell bumped into a cat named Mike, who he barely remembered, but apparently Mike recognized him.

"What up, gawd!" Mike said attempting to give Brezell dap, but he didn't return the dap. He just nodded his head and kept it moving. Mike felt a bit offended from his facial expression, but brushed off his anger and again attempted to befriend Brezell. However, Brezell was not one of those friendly ass niggas. Mike seemed as grimy as Brezell was so his kissing Brezell's ass was suspect.

Brezell knew off top, in any other circumstances, Mike would've tried to fight, which led him to believe he was on something and didn't have time for him to mess up his plans.

"What up, B, I see you don't remember a nigga." Mike said in efforts to make conversation.

Brezell strained his eyes as if he were trying to remember.

"From where?" Brezell asked suspiciously.

"From my manz and 'em. Seven, ya NY people; them my peoples. I met you when you slid through awhile back," he said, holding his arms out to show he didn't mean any harm.

"Word?" Brezell stated in question.

"Yeah, I'm surprised you don't remember me. I came through Chi-town with my guy on a humbug and I remember Quita introducing us to you."

"Quita?" Brezell was starting to think the nigga had him mixed up.

"Seven's home girl out in Chi. Thick lil chick, from the boogie down; lil gutta type ho," Mike added.

"You talking about Sheila?" he asked, becoming irritated.

"Ahh, yeah, Sheila, that's her," Mike fronted. "Yo son, run a check through my nigga, Seven. Take my number and holla at me if you trying to bus some moves." Mike said trying to play it cool.

"Awight dawg, I got you. I'mma lock that number in and get at you, *if* I'm interested," Brezell said ready to step.

Mike was a known stick up kid. Brezell heard that when times got rough, he burned bridges with all the local money getters so he had to travel outside of home to make moves. He didn't think twice about calling Mike, he just wanted to get the nigga out of his grill so he could pop a bottle of that Ace of Spade and party like a rock star.

The set up...

Damn, I hope that nigga call. I need this out of town lick, Mike mumbled to himself as he walked away from Brezell. He didn't really give a fuck, he just wanted to get money, fuck the dumb shit. He kept in touch with a chi-town bust down, Brea. Eagerly, she had given him the nigga's blueprint and the full run down of his business while Mike visited Chicago months before. He knew Brezell was getting money, but he had no idea to what extent until Seven casually confirmed it. Little did Brezell know Mike had plans for him to be his star player. As soon as he got a chance, Mike called Brea.

"What up, ma?" he asked her.

"Who dis?" Brea questioned.

"Damn lil momma, a nigga up here thinking about you and you don't even know my voice?" he teased her.

"Aww, what's up NY, my bad," she said recognizing his accent. Mike made casual talk before bringing up what he really called for.

"I saw ya mans up here in the club the other day," he said slyly.

"Who?" Brea questioned, thinking that he better not say Brezell because he promised to take her on the next trip to New York.

"Ya man Brezell," Mike stated. "He was wit some chicken head, trying to disguise herself for classy."

Brea was secretly jealous, but didn't want it to show so she attempted to change the subject.

"What's been up with you though? When you coming back this way to lay that dick down?" she said seductively.

"That's what's up ma, when you want me to come?" he asked her.

"Whenever, I'm not fucking wit nobody like that so come when you want," she lied, knowing Brezell had claims on her. She planned to make him jealous; she knew how stingy he was with the pussy he made claims on.

"Awight, but I need you to do me a favor, ma." Mike was planning to use her too.

"What's that, G?" she quizzed.

"Yo little gang banging ass is funny. I need you to put in a good word for me with that nigga Brezell, let him know I'm getting money so that nigga will fuck wit me on that work tip. Set something up kid, you know what to say. I'mma hit you off wit some dough if that nigga fuck wit me. I fucks wit you, boo, so I trust you to get a nigga plugged." Mike knew she would go for the bait with her money hungry ass.

"I got you, Money Mike. Hit me up next week than, ok. Peace."

They hung up with different motives. Mike wanted to come out to Chicago and bust a move on Brezell with hopes of fleeing with plenty of loot. Brea wanted to use Mike to make Brezell jealous since she was green that he had another chick out of town with him.

Yeah, I'm going to show Breezy he ain't the only one that I can fuck wit' having money. I'm gone fuck wit' his supplier and make that nigga, mad. Brezell really gon' be fuming, she thought vindictively to herself.

Immediately upon returning to Chicago, Karma and Brezell parted ways. Karma wanted to get business back in order at her shop and he had dealings of his own. He made his rounds as usual. They brought a few bricks back in the car, but the rest would be sent to Karma's hair shop as hair supplies. Karma had done a good job of keeping their affair on the down low. She knew Brezell was a very sought after man and didn't need the drama. She asked him to keep it quiet as well.

"Look, keep this low, alright."

Kamara wanted to tell her mom, Komara, since she dated his fake ass dad, but held back on that for the time being. Their private affair was a well-kept secret.

On his grind, Brezell didn't tell anybody when he would be back; he had a few days before he would need to hook up with Karma again to receive the shipment. Meanwhile, he wanted to pop up to Sheila's apartment first and surprise her. However, he was the one surprised when he saw Dean's car in front of the apartment. Brezell parked his Masaridi in the underground parking, connected to the apartment complex so he was able to enter directly through the building. He snuck in with the key Sheila gave him and neither heard him come in.

Sheila laid there naked, puffing on a black and mild cigar while Dean was taking a shower. Brezell walked in and she almost passed out. He saw guilt all over her face so he already knew something was up. Not to mention, empty condom wrappers were on the floor. Sheila just sat there in shock; speechless. He gave her the evil eye as he walked to open the door of the bathroom where Dean bathed. He peeked his head in and observed Dean happily showering, unaware of the danger awaiting him.

"Let me explain!" Sheila began to stutter. Brezell was so heated; he punched Sheila in the stomach so hard that her bowels gave out.

"You trifling bitch, I'm through fucking wit you. You wanna be a whore, than go ahead 'cause I don't need you."

Before Brezell could continue pounding on Sheila, Dean came out the bathroom with a towel wrapped around his waist without looking up and said, "Ready for round three?"

Sheila couldn't do nothing but howl. Brezell stood ready to charge. Dean finally noticed him and his eyes almost popped out his head.

Diary of a Kingpin's Daughter

"You like hitting my snatch, huh, nigga?" Brezell questioned.

"It's not like that man, she called me. She says she didn't fuck wit' you anymore. I..I...um, really just came to see my son," Dean stumbled over his words. "When I got here, she got to talking about us getting back together shit."

Brezell almost lost his balance. "Ya son?" he asked confused.

"Yeah, she told me the lil' nigga was mine. At first she didn't know for sure so we took a blood test recently and it came back 99.9% positive," he stated almost shaking of fright. He knew as well as Sheila did that Brezell had clout and could make them both disappear.

"You know what, I'm not mad at you player cause it's not your fault, it's this ho's fault for not knowing who her baby's daddy is. I'm gonna give you a ghetto pass this time and let you leave while I handle my business with this slut," Brezell fumed glaring at Sheila.

Dean was so petrified that he scooped his clothes up off the floor and ran off.

"Sheila, I'll get lil' man from the neighbors."

Brezell said in return, "Yeah, you betta handle that 'cause he gon' at least need a daddy. This bitch is a done deal."

▶ ▶ ▶ ▶ ▶

Detective Stark sat in a car in clear view of the apartment building. Seeing a young man run out with a towel hanging from his body caught his eye. He watched closely to see what or who would come running out in pursuit. He knew Brezell went into underground parking, but was unsure of which apartment he went inside of once out of the garage. So, he decided to lurk the hallway in case this strange flee was connected to Brezell's visit. He stood in the hall extra quiet but suddenly heard piercing screams coming from Apartment #2. He dialed 911 on his cell phone and proceeded to bang on the door to assist the screaming person. Detective Stark was hot on Brezell's trail and determined to bring him down. Since he knew Brezell had dealings with Sheila, she was the first in line for questioning and he hoped she wasn't the woman who'd finally stopped screaming.

Brezell heard the knocks and got nervous, thinking Dean must have called the Po-Po on him. He grabbed his coat and ran out the back door. Sheila remained spread across the bed, unconscious, and covered in her own blood and feces. Brezell didn't want to run outside and risk being seen leaving the crime scene, so he ran through the back door of Brea's apartment. Brea heard the commotion through the thin walls so she immediately knew whom to expect behind the urgent knocks. As soon as she opened the door, Brezell franticly closed and locked it.

Although Brea was still upset from their last conversation when she found out that Brezell went to New York without her, by the look on his face she knew now wasn't the time for her nagging. She had yet to encounter the wrath of the devil's child.

"What's going on?" Brea shouted afraid that someone was going to come busting in behind him.

"The bitch lost her mind. She over there fucking and sucking some nigga who claim to be my son's daddy, then got the nerve to try and explain. I would feel less of a man if I walked out of there without putting hands on that gutter snipe. I ain't no ho ass nigga. You just don't do shit like that and think I'm gone let that shit ride!" Brezell shouted, almost out of breath from running. He knew he had hurt Sheila badly because after the last blow to the face, she wasn't moving. And he didn't show any remorse for Sheila.

"So she called the police on you?"

"Naw, some nosey muthafucka knocked so I ran over here and if anybody asks, you haven't seen me and you didn't hear anything," he demanded.

"Hear no evil, see no evil. I ain't got nothing to do with that," Brea assured.

"Go run me some bath water," he insisted. He always thought a hot bath would calm him and for now that would do until things settled down a bit.

▶ ▶ ▶ ▶ ▶

When the police arrived, they knocked on several doors trying to get answers. Brezell left Sheila for dead and no one knew anything, but Brea and Dean. However, Brea had covered Brezell until the ambulance and the detectives left the area. Dean was no where to be found and Sheila was clinging to life.

When the smoke cleared, Brezell left and being nosey, Brea decided to visit Sheila in the hospital. During her visit, she learned that Sheila's lungs collapsed and she had two broken ribs. Brea's chest caved in when she saw Sheila lying there half-breathing.

Damn! I wouldn't wish this on my worst enemy. Breezy fucked her up. She thought in guilt.

Brea just couldn't believe he beat her that bad. She sat by Sheila's side and shed tears.

"Girl, I'm sorry. I know I fucked you over, but regardless of that shit, I should've helped you. I am so sorry." She wept.

The nurse walked in and interrupted her private confession.

"Oh, I apologize. I didn't mean to bother you," the nurse stated.

"It's cool," Brea said, in a whisper wiping her tears.

"Are you a relative?" the nurse inquired.

"Something like that. I'm her best friend." She fabricated.

"Good, the doctors, as well as the police, have been trying to contact relatives and friends of this poor girl." The nursed said, in a sympathetic tone. She handed Brea a card with the officer assigned to the case with a number on it. "The Officer told me to give this card to anyone who came to visit. I'll be right back." She left out the room with the doctor that had been caring for Sheila.

"Nice to meet you. Can you answer any medical questions for your best friend? Do you know if she's allergic to anything or, if she has a family history of medical conditions?"

Brea looked at him with empathetic eyes and lied potentially causing future risks for Sheila.

"No. You know what this is a bit much for me. Let me try to contact her family and have them help you. I'll be sure to contact the Officer, too." Brea jetted out the hospital as fast as she could.

After the visit, she contacted Mike in New York to inform him of what happened.

"Mike, you better get the fuck down here! That nigga Breezy done went crazy and tried to kill Sheila. I wanted to help the bitch, but he even pushed me down. You know I ran like crazy. Yeah, yeah, you and Seven need to get here like ASAP! You know he's holding."

Brea promised herself to stay as far away from Brezell as possible; seeing Sheila had scared her straight. Well, almost, she figured if she let Mike and Seven handle Brezell, this would be her revenge to him for all his lies and games towards her. Plus, she felt cheated because he wasn't cashing out like he promised. She knew Seven and Mike would throw her something for looking out.

"Yo, we on the next thing smokin'," Mike gladly informed her.

Mike was very pleased that Seven had finally agreed to let him strip Brezell of all of his material wealth. He was always the type of cat who wanted things to come easy. Instead of working hard or hustling good to get it, he'd rather someone else put in the hard work so he could just take it. And he was as gutter as they came; Shyster was his middle name and there were only a few people he wouldn't fuck over. Brezell wasn't one of them. To him, he flossed too hard and had to get it.

In less than six hours, Mike and Seven were in Chicago ready to wreck shop.

"Son, you know I'ma kill the guy, right?" Mike stated to Seven.

"Murder, man? Let's just play it by ear, check wit' Quita and go from there. If ma cool and she make it through, I'll consider letting the lil nigga live," Seven said, blowing out his cigarette smoke.

"Yeah aii'right," Mike replied, with his eyes at the top of his head.

Fresh off the plane, they connected with Brea. Brea gave up all the tapes. The name to every hang out and address that she knew of on Brezell, which included Karma's spot, Bionca's crib, and Money Green's houses.

"The only address I don't know is where him and his wife live. All the rest of the places are legit. He frequents all of them."

The first place the police investigated after leaving the hospital was the home Brezell and Chloe still shared. At first Chloe was uncooperative until the police produced pictures of Sheila. Her circumstances would bring anybody to their knees.

"Mrs. Wright it's very important that you talk to us. We have reason to believe your husband Brezell is responsible for committing this crime and others." Detective Stark explained to Chloe.

"But why? Who is this girl? And, what other crimes?" Chloe responded, distraught.

"We have a star witness that indicated Brezell is trafficking cocaine. And, we also have reason to believe that your husband is possibly involved in the death of your parents." He answered regretfully.

Chloe's heart stopped. Devastated wasn't the feeling. Not one word could describe her feelings at this point. Her stomach instantly tied itself in a double knot. She already felt this man stripped her of her integrity. Not to mention, constantly threatened her life, as well as, the life of their unborn child. To find out it was a possibility that he'd taken her mother and father out was way too much to grasp. She sat attentively clinging to Detective Stark's, every word.

"I don't know what to believe. I don't think he could do..." she began, but busted out in tears. "What do you need me to do?"

"Allow us to bug your home. Listen, if we find anything that would incriminate you, we will grant you full immunity if you let us do this. Otherwise, you'll go down with him if we get a search warrant for this house and find drugs and guns. I'm sure you know, there's a gun or two, maybe even drugs in here." Detective Stark let that sink in. "I see that you're pregnant, too. You don't want to deliver your baby in Federal prison, do you? So, what's it going to be?"

"O, O, Okay," she agreed. Now in other circumstances, she would have stuck by the street code and rode it out with her man, but not in this case. If he was a suspect in her mother and father's murder, fuck him! She had her own personal vendetta with the man that she promised before God to love through sickness and health; till death did them part. It wasn't about the drugs; it was about the murder of her mother and father.

The big pay back

Brezell and Bionca lay high as a kite from smoking, popping ecstasy pills, and snorting cocaine, which was her idea of him showing love. Bionca sent the baby to her father's, house for a few days, per Brezell's request. Since John Otis' death, her dad was flying straight like most of JO's old crew. He was settling down as a grandfather and living off of his investments. He told Bionca things could never be the same, real niggas were a rare breed and hard to come by so with that in mind, he decided to retire from the game and fall back.

Instead of knocking, someone kicked hard at Bionca's door, scaring the shit out of them. Brezell immediately said to say he wasn't there, regardless of who it was. Before she went to the door, Bionca watched him hide securely in case the police wanted to walk through the house. Opening the door, she was relieved it wasn't the police and automatically began to snap out.

"What the fuck? You muthafuckas ain't got no sense, beatin' my damn door like that!" She glared at them with glossy, red eyes.

Seven began to laugh at her. "Yo, Mike, this bitch is high. What's good, ma?"

Mike joined in on the amusement, "Baby girl, wipe ya nose boo, you got powder all around ya shit."

The two men cackled hysterically.

"Fuck you niggas, get the hell off of my door step!" Bionca screamed attempting to slam the door.

Mike put his foot in the way and in one movement, slapped her to the floor.

"Crab ass slut, don't you ever disrespect a Gawd like that! Now, where dat grimy ass nigga of yours at?" he questioned.

Now afraid for her life, Bionca wasn't about to tell. Even though she didn't have a clue to what was going on, she wasn't about to give up her time with Brezell for nobody, even if it meant dying. She didn't care what happened to her as long as she lived to be loved by him. Down on the floor with a throbbing face, she continued to talk to them disrespectfully.

"Fuck you! I dunno where dat nigga at, you find him!" Bionca hollered getting up off the floor.

Seven let out an easy chuckle listening to Bionca. "Damn son, you can't even keep the bitch off her feet!" he laughed at Mike.

Turning his attention back to her, Seven got serious.

"Look here ho, next time, shit ain't gon' be so sweet. Tell ya boy to holla at Seven. You tell 'im we'll be at Split Endz waiting for him."

Mike smacked Bionca on the ass and the two departed without knowing Brezell was right in the house.

Brezell listened to the whole thing in a cold sweat; afraid they would hear him breathing. He figured they would come for him, but he didn't expect it to be so soon. He knew Money Mike was on him. As soon as he was sure they left, he came from his hiding place trying to conceal his nervousness. Now, not only did he have to duck and dodge the police, but Mike and Seven as well.

"What the fuck is going on, Brezell?" Bionca questioned.

"Bitch, shut up and mind your own damn business sometimes!" he shouted attempting to get dressed. Brezell was so high that he didn't know which way to go. He put his shirt on inside out.

Bionca stood staggered. She knew not to go there with him, not now anyway. So, she did as he said and shut up while watching him pace for a few minutes not knowing what his next move was. He knew Mike and Seven were already on their way to Karma's. There was a fresh shipment waiting for pick up and Brezell was sure they'd get that.

Without thinking, Brezell blurted out, "If I said come on, let's move out of state tomorrow, what would you say, B?" he asked Bionca seriously.

"What time you want me to be ready, baby!" she smiled pleased.

"You think yo pops will keep lil J-dub for a little while?"

"With no problem," she smiled.

She was leaving with her man and nothing was going to stop her, not even her own son.

Satisfied with her answer, Brezell kissed her in the mouth; something he rarely did.

"Go get that powder so you can suck it off of daddy's dick," he instructed her referring to the cocaine. Just like an obedient ho, she did what she was told.

Bionca was slowly dying on the inside and with his help she was digging her own grave. She was no longer the vibrant, fine, bombshell she was as a teen. She was on her way to being a full-blown cokehead.

After she sucked Brezell dry, he left with the objective to return to Bionca so the two of them could attempt to change areas codes. First, he had to gather some belongings from home.

As soon as Mike and Seven attempted to pull up to Split Endz, they seen the place was surrounded by the law.

"Damn, nigga. They beat us to the punch. Let's go check for Quita." Seven sighed.

Karma was presently being held by the U.S. Marshals for ties to Brezell's drug ring, weekly shipments signed off by her. The officials knew all about the shipments of work she stored as beauty supplies for Brezell. However, she wasn't going out like that. Karma started singing all she could about Brezell to assure her own freedom. Komara and Monte were already on the first flight back from Houston, TX to be by Karma's side. Monte barely had concern for his son. He knew from the start Brezell was on the road to self-destruction so he allowed fate to take its course. It was just a matter of time before doom caught up to him.

When Brezell got to his house, his goal was to creep in the house unseen and unheard to grab the money that he secretly hid in the walls. He planned to escape to a new existence in another state with his long-term mistress. This shit was getting too hot and too complicated. Things definitely didn't work out the way he planned.

Trying to sneak in the house, Brezell was never expecting Chloe to be wandering the house, awaiting his arrival. She couldn't sleep after hearing the accusations concerning the death of her parents. Her objective was to play it cool and help lead the police to an arrest, but seeing Brezell's face brought about an infuriated rage.

She instantly attacked, biting, scratching, kicking, and doing whatever to illustrate her hurt and fury. Although her stomach was round and full-figured her blows continued to come in remorse.

"I hate you, I hate you!" she shouted between swings.

With no regard to the baby or her, for that matter, Brezell put all his might into his punch and knocked her down. Without saying a word, he stepped over her bemused body and continued on his mission. Brezell didn't waste any time punching holes in the wall, directly above where he had the money stored. When they first bought the condo, he hired a company to come in and create a safe hiding space behind the plaster. He didn't want to risk anyone finding it. He knew a safe or hidden compartment wasn't that hard to locate. Chloe lay on the floor dazed and in pain. She had shooting pains running from her neck to her stomach. Of all the times he'd hit her, even doing extensive damages that she never mentioned to anyone, this time she felt he would pay. Thoughts of her family appeared in her head as well as all the drama Brezell put her through. For the last few days, the streets had been talking. She had to confirm what the police had been telling her for herself. It's amazing how powerful street gossip could be and all she had to do was ask the right person. She found out lots of facts about both his children, as well as the full low down on the other baby momma, Shelia. It was even rumored that Karma may have been carrying his seed, which wasn't surprising because this nigga loved it raw.

Trying to shake off her daze, Chloe stumbled into the room where they kept a .380-millimeter gun. With no remorse, Brezell pulled the black Fendi duffle bag from the wall. Smiling to himself, he peaked in the bag and inhaled the fresh money scent. He hadn't considered Chloe retaliating. She stood in stance near the front door, watching him and waiting on her opponent. Brezell didn't take the standoff seriously; he thought she was too pathetic to pull the trigger by the way her hands trembled.

"Why Brezell, why did you kill my parents?" she bawled with blood running down her face and legs.

"Just move out the way and you'll never have to worry about me again a day in your life, I promise," he said, very flatly. His distress was elsewhere; he didn't consider her a threat.

"I thought you loved me? First, you murder the most important people in my life and now you're just gonna walk out on me, just like that?" she cocked the gun ready to fire. "You think it's that easy? I'll kill you before I let this shit ride," she shouted.

"Girl, you talking crazy. Move your ass from in front of the door before I give you one to the dome, like I did your mother!" he exposed.

The police had been listening the entire time and felt with that statement, he confessed to the murders and it was time to intervene. The knocks at the door broke Chloe's concentration allowing Brezell a chance to grab for the gun.

They tussled to the floor, neither loosening their grip. Chloe began to feel faint as Brezell put his knee in her stomach. In reflex, she pulled the trigger.

Hearing the gunshot, the police began to kick the door in.

Blood splashed in Chloe's eyes, blurring her vision. Although she could not see, she felt Brezell's hands tighten around her neck. Without a second thought, she pulled the trigger again and this time he lay motionless. The floor was covered in Brezell's blood and fluid – Chloe's fluid – her water broke.

"Mrs. Wright!" The official called out upon entering the house.

Chloe was too weak to respond. Immediately they ran to her side. Medical help was already on the way. Unsure of who was shot, they checked each one of their pulse. She made a few groans to show life while Brezell showed none.

Detective Stark arrived shortly after. The police were afraid to move Chloe so they gently wiped her face with a cold towel. Blood and fluid trickled down her legs and she knew this meant danger for the baby. She prayed that God could again spare the life of the innocence she held inside of her. She made two requests before they rushed her off to the hospital. She requested for the administrators to contact her cousin, Squeak, and for someone to bring her hospital bag, which she described as a black Fendi duffle bag sitting by the door. Without hesitation Detective Stark, did as asked and headed for the hospital without suspension or question.

Every dog has its day...

Brezell and Chloe were both in the hospital. Brezell lay in critical condition with an immovable bullet in his lungs and a wound in his stomach and left side. He had been given a blood transfusion and his kidneys were failing. The doctors recommended a family member step up to donate blood and possibly a kidney. Chloe had to get an emergency c-section. Although she was only 6 ½ months, the baby had a better chance to live if delivered early.

▶ ▶ ▶ ▶ ▶

Monte reached the hospital with butterflies in his stomach. He knew his paternity secret was sure to be exposed when he and Brezell took the blood tests. Monte was going to act surprised when the blood didn't come back a match. Right now, he cared more for Chloe's well-being than Brezell's. He secretly hoped Brezell wouldn't make it out of surgery; he felt life would be better this way. He knew Brezell was a menace to society and burden in all of their lives.

▶ ▶ ▶ ▶ ▶

Squeak, Jade, and Aunt Ryan waited patiently in the family waiting room for the okay to visit Chloe. The power of technology along with skillful doctors and the grace of God, Nakima Jocelle Carter was born 4 pounds 9 ounces premature, but she would make it with the help of a breathing machine and good nurturing.

The family was allowed to visit Chloe, but the baby had to remain in an incubator in the nursery. Chloe's face was swollen, aching, and busied; her body was sore, but she was alive and talking.

Detective Stark dropped off the bag and mouthed to her, "You owe me."

"Grab that bag, Squeak." Chloe motioned, pointing to the chair where Detective Stark left it. "Go 'head and open it."

Squeak's mouth fell open when she looked inside the bag.

"Oww, oww, shit!" Squeak screamed, looking over at Jade and Aunt Ryan.

"Keep it quiet. How much is in it?" Chloe calmly asked.

"Girl, you are not gone believe this! It's a bag full of money wrapped in plastic. And it's an old, beat up diary and some bank papers in here too," she added, leaning the bag over so Chloe could see.

"How much money you think it is?" Chloe asked, again.

Squeak unwrapped a stack of bills and counted them.

"This one by itself is a thousand dollars, so when you get a chance and more privacy, you can count each by packs and total it. You don't want to do it now cause if someone walks in on us counting all this money, too many questions will arise," Squeak commented.

"You're right," she agreed, "but let me see the diary and the bank papers."

Chloe reviewed the bank papers in astonishment.

"That nigga really planned on running off in the sunset. According to these papers, he had Diddy-type money stashed overseas; his ass was just gone bounce on me like Mase!"

Squeak laughed, "Sucks to be him cause he'll never get to it, instead of rapping about mo money, mo problems, he'll be singing, 'No money, don't come around, my baby momma shot me and I can't see'!"

The ladies cracked up, but Chloe didn't laugh.

In fact, that was a very sensitive subject to her and she wasn't ready to talk or joke about it yet. Her main priority at the time was her baby girl struggling to hold on to dear life.

Squeak knew she was out of line so she quickly apologized. "I'm sorry Chloe, but I'm trying to make light outta a fucked up situation, feel me?"

The nurse buzzed the room to ask if Chloe wanted to visit the baby in the nursery.

"Yes, thank you." She stashed the papers back in the bag and put it back under her bed.

Aunt Ryan assisted her into her robe while Squeak and Jade waited outside the room.

"Aunt Ryan, do you think my baby girl will be okay?"

"Sure, she will. If she's anything like the Carter's, she'll be just fine."

"I feel so stupid. I want to cry right now. He used me, Auntie. How fucked up is that? Would you have known? Or, was I too damn blind?"

"Nah, baby. You weren't blind. That nigga had us all fooled. I truly thought he loved you and I'm sure JO and Kim did, too."

Aunt Ryan helped ease Chloe down in the wheel chair and kissed her on her cheek before rolling her to the nursery.

Before visiting her angel, Chloe had to cover her mouth with a doctor's mask and gloves to assure no germs would get to the baby. She was unable to hold her at the time; all she could do was stick her hands through a small hole in the incubator and touch her daughter's tiny body gently. The sight of her infant had Chloe more emotional and she began to cry. Squeak was right by her side to comfort her.

"She's my miracle baby, Squeak. The last couple of months have been hell. I'm surprised she even came out alive and well!" Chloe wept.

"Brezell man-handled me, beating me like it wasn't shit and every time, he'd tell me to call on my daddy for help, knowing he was gone." She covered her face in humiliation.

"It's okay." Squeak embraced her tightly. "He'll never hurt you again, I promise you that."

"You know what? I should wish that nigga was dead right now, but that's not in me. He'll get his, fa' sure."

"You damn right about that!" Aunt Ryan yelled.

▶ ▶ ▶ ▶ ▶

As Monte prepared for the blood work to be done he reminded himself to come off surprised when the test revealed he wasn't the biological father to Brezell.

"Mr. Wright, we're going to prep your son for surgery and as long as your blood type matches, he should be good to go with a very slow recovery." The doctor spoke to him.

"Okay, keep me posted." He said, as he gave a weak and phony smile. *That'll never happen, cause the DNA won't match,* Monte thought to himself.

Komara and Monte set a wedding date and after tying the rest of their loose ends in Chicago, they planned to never turn back. The fast life may have brought about fast money, fast cars, and fast women, but it mostly brought about an express ticket to an early grave, which Monte wanted no parts of. His main concern was his future wife and his daughter, Cashay, who was due to graduate from college soon. His last hopes were with his daughter not his son.

Monte personally felt like he failed Brezell as a man, but still had his little girl to steer correctly. He was proud that she had a new life in Houston and didn't consider moving back to Chicago.

▶ ▶ ▶ ▶ ▶

Seven and Mike sat by Sheila's side in hopes that she would come to. Seven was satisfied that Brezell got what he had coming, but in Mike's opinion he felt Brezell got off too easy.

"A coward dies a thousand deaths!" Seven assured Mike.

"Go on wit' all that Tupac ass shit, B! I wanted to be the one to send that nigga to his maker." Mike grimaced.

Seven promised that if Sheila pulled through this, he would take her and her son back to New York and make sure she lived comfortable in her own hometown. He took responsibility for what happened to her. He put her in the game and he helped her flee her hometown. If he would have just paid a good lawyer for her in the first place, she could've stayed in NY and none of this would have went down like it had. But instead, she took on another identity and her life took a turn for the worst. The thought of her dying ate at Seven, painfully. Over time, he had grown to love her like a sister.

▶ ▶ ▶ ▶ ▶

With Karma in jail and Brezell on his deathbed, Brea laid low hoping for the best. She feared the Feds would come pick her up for information. She didn't wish death on anybody, but Brezell's death was worth $300,000 to her in life insurance money so, again, Brea hoped for the worst. If he did pass, she planned to be on the first thing smoking to Los Angeles where she could buy a new life with the money. If not, there were plenty of moneymakers she could scheme off of in L.A. After all, one monkey didn't stop her show.

▶ ▶ ▶ ▶ ▶

Karma prayed the lawyer Monte sent for her was a damn good one. She had already set her mind to tell whatever information needed to clear her own ass. There was a lot of evidence being held against her; from phone conversations, to the recent shipment of drugs sent to Split Endz that she signed for, to the trip to New York. Not to mention a long list of things purchased with drug money. It was just her luck that the surveillance started when she decided to join the team.

Komara felt like karma had literally came back to bite them both in the ass. The chase for the mighty dollar was coming to an end and neither one of them had won the race.

Karma hoped Brezell would pull through. Not because she cared, but because if he didn't, she would be charged for his crimes. She was facing 30 to life for Kingpin charges, Trafficking, Conspiracy, Possession and any other charge they could give her related to drugs. She would have to take the rap for it all, especially since the packages were sent in her name.

Detective Stark was very pleased that the blood in BG's fingernails matched the DNA of Brezell's. BG had since come out of his comatose state and was willing to testify. His motor skills and some of his body functions would take some time and intense therapy before he would be his normal self again, if ever. He was in total awe when the story came together in his mind. It saddened him deeply of his mere association with the deaths of Mr. and Mrs. Carter. It ate at him so much he agreed to help bring Brezell down with his indictment. The realization that the street life wasn't for him had finally set in.

Detective Stark may have been the second person wishing for Brezell to survive, but only to have him rot in jail for the rest of his life.

Final judgment...

Chloe sat in her room alone and reflected on all of the events that had occurred in her life. She thought about the decisions she made and how by the change of a simple thought, her life would have turned out different. She had given her parents a granddaughter, whom they would never meet. She knew if her father were still alive he would be so disappointed in her. She made up her mind to return to school and get a degree. At least they would've been proud of her for that.

Chloe couldn't sleep so she decided to go through the diary that was stored in the duffle bag. Opening it up it read, *This diary belongs to Mrs. Tina Wright.*

She stayed up all night reading through the memoirs of Brezell's mother. This was definitely a tell-all. She got to the part that concerned her father and the affairs he had kept with Tina over the years. She scanned the pages fixatedly as her chest caved in. She couldn't believe what she was reading. This couldn't be true; it was written that her husband was actually her half-brother.

Chloe started hyperventilating, unable to control her breathing. Things were starting to fall into place. Brezell's comments as well as most of his bizarre behaviors were starting to make sense. Their entire relationship had been a lie; their marriage was the start to his ambush on her life.

This couldn't be happening.

She dropped the diary in disgust and strived to gain her composure.

"God, why?" She cried out to the air. "What did I ever do to deserve this life?"

Chloe wondered who else knew of this dreadful disgusting secret as embarrassment and anger tortured her soul. She requested extra pain medication and allowed that to place her into a deep sleep. She hoped to wake up and it would all be one big, bad dream.

▶ ▶ ▶ ▶ ▶

Bionca remained secluded in her home a nervous, drugged-up wreck. She prayed for Brezell to make it out okay because, in her mind, she couldn't live without him. For days, she sat in the house snorting the cocaine he left behind, numbing herself of the pain and the reality of life. She was half-insane by this time; she hadn't bathed herself or eaten anything since she heard what happened to Brezell. She was too out of it to even visit him. She had no intentions of sending for her son, her father could have him for all she cared. All she wanted was Brezell. She revolved her life around his every being and wasn't prepared to be without him.

▶ ▶ ▶ ▶ ▶

"Hello, Mr. Wright, this is Dr. Jeffery Coleman, the doctor treating your son," he announced, through the telephone.

"Hi, how are you?" Monte answered attentively anticipating the news that the blood type didn't match.

"I just wanted to inform you that we're prepping your son for surgery and afterwards, he'll be in recovery for at least five hours. After that, it'll be okay to visit him."

Monte's heart dropped. "O-okay," he stated confused.

"Do you have any questions?" the doctored asked sensing something was wrong.

"Honestly doc, I wasn't sure if I was the natural father and I wasn't expecting the DNA to match," he acknowledged hesitantly.

"Just to assure you, sir, it is hospital policy to test for a match, and the results were favorable. That's as precise as one can get. You have nothing to worry about. I'll see you in a few hours," the doctor confirmed before closing the conversation and saying good bye.

Brezell laid in recovery mode, drowsy from all the medication. He couldn't feel a muscle in his body. He blinked his eyes a few times to focus his vision. At first he was unsure of where he was. He wiggled his toes and then his fingers. He slowly remembered the past day's events. He pictured the bright flash from the gunshots that caught him in the neck, stomach, and side. He attempted to speak, but was interrupted by the tubes that went from his nose down his throat. All he could think about was what he was going do to Chloe once he recovered.

I'm gone kill the bitch this time, just like I did her punk ass daddy, Brezell thought to himself.

He had plans to skip town as soon as he was discharged from the hospital. His thoughts were interrupted by a gentle knock on the door.

Brezell glanced up, still in thought.

"Jonathan, I'm glad to see you've awakened. I'm Dr. Wedderburn, the attending physician for ICU, where you have been unconscious for a few days. You have your father to thank for your life," he continued. "You lost a lot of blood and have undergone two blood transfusions and your dad willingly gave you exactly what you needed."

Brezell was in shock, he couldn't respond, instead he screwed up his face up to show his bitterness. He hoped this wouldn't happen to be the Dr. Wedderburn that was BG's father. If so, he prayed that he didn't have any knowledge of his involvement with his son since his life was in his hands.

"I don't know if you would've survived if your father wasn't a perfect match. That's the least of your worries now though. You have a stack of Detectives and Police Officers waiting for you to get well. Once released and in police custody, you'll need this colostomy bag temporarily."

Brezell closed his eyes in disgust. When he opened them, he laid his eyes upon his father.

Immediately entering the room, Monte had bad vibes just from being in Brezell's presence.

"Son," he said sarcastically.

Brezell stared with an aggrieved expression to show his disapproval of the visit.

"Let me keep this brief. I know how you truly feel about me, as well as how your mother did. I know about the diary and your intentions to get revenge for your mother."

Brezell's eyes grew wide at the mention of the diary.

"I know all that you know, Brezell. And I can live with that, but you have to live with the fact that you ruined lots of lives in vain. I no longer give a fuck about how you feel about me. I spent years trying to figure out why you and your mom had so much resentment for me when all I did was care for my family. You know you took JO and Kim out for nothing? Man, I knew for years about your mother and JO, but I never tried to do them harm. You know shit has a way of coming back to you. Nigga, you done. The Feds after you and you're facing hella time. They have been investigating you, nigga, not me so I'm clean as far as they know. Don't even think about trying to pull me down with you. Let's see you get yourself out of this one, H.N.I.C. That's what you wanted to be, right?" Monte laughed savagely. "If you've never honored anything I said, respect this, live by the sword, and die by the sword, nigga!"

Monte said his piece and silently walked out on his only son, vowing to never look back. His focus was on the second chance he was given.

▶ ▶ ▶ ▶ ▶

"Quita!" Seven shook her. "Come on, Quita. You gotta pull through this." He managed to say peering from the flat line that appeared on the screen.

"Fuck nigga, she dead. We gotta bounce, now!" Mike vexed.

"Damn! Peace, Quita. R.I.P., baby." Seven choked up leaving her behind.

Arrangements were being made for her body to be shipped back to New York. Dean got custody of their son and immediately filed a petition to change his name. Seven and Mike returned to New York, where they planned to give Marquita "Sheila" Coleman the proper burial. Seven's heart weighed heavily on her death. He promised to help provide for her children to any extent for as long as he was able.

Last words...

Dear Diary,

    This last year has been one of the worst periods of my life, but I'm not complaining because out of it, I received my ultimate blessing; my daughter, Nakima Jocelle Carter. Hell no, I didn't give her that fuck nigga's last name. I was fucked up when I found out Brezell could've possibly been my brother. How fucked up is that? Thank God Monte assured me that he wasn't. Can you imagine that nasty shit? I'm still trying to figure out if Brezell believed he was my brother, how could he come to fuck me in the first place? Bugged out ass crazy, nigga!

    All of my bumps and bruises may have healed, but I know I will never fully mend from all of the pain and hurt he inflicted on me. He's in jail and may never meet freedom again. Although he took my family away from me, I send flicks of Nakima to him. I make sure not to put a return address on them though. And damn if she don't look just like him, but I call her Jo-Jo because her little attitude reminds me of daddy.

    Out of all the women Brezell cheated on me with, I wonder how many of them keep in contact with him now. Probably none of them ho's 'cause they never truly cared in the first place. I guess in this game no one can truly be trusted. Those I thought were my friends wore enemies in camouflage. I heard Karma was stripped of her shop, seeing as how she had no proof of income to prove she didn't open and operate it with drug money. She was spared jail time due to her testimony against Brezell. They granted her immunity just like they did me. Her involvement with my husband didn't surprise me. Any bitch game for fast money was on him. I can't really knock their hustle. I just hate that I had to be the victim. Guess what, that bitch Bionca running around selling ass and whatever else to get her next hit. Mr. Juan was given full custody of her poor son. Out of the kindness of my heart, I send what I can to help contribute to the care of my daughter's older half-brother. Eventually, I do plan to allow the two a normal sibling relationship. They're innocent in all the havoc. I wouldn't want them to cross paths later in life and be clueless to their kinship.

In due time, Jo-Jo will be told the story of her parent's life, but only when she's able to fully understand. I especially wouldn't want little Jonathan or Brezell seeking revenge on their own sister because the affect the mayhem has had on each of their lives.

As for Brea, I hear she's still on the prowl for an easy come up.

There were so many lives affected by Brezell.

Diary of a Kingpin's Daughter

Along with the help of a little therapy and my favorite cousin, Squeak, I'm going on with my life and I'm living it to the fullest, not taking a moment for granted. That money that was in the duffel bag, I let Squeak and Aunt Ryan split that. They were happier than a mothafucka.

I already had stacks of legitimate money. So when the Feds came to seize the house and cars, it didn't faze me. I left without argument. That house held nothing but bad memories for me anyway. I'm now living in an undisclosed location in a different state, which I won't even mention to you, although you are my diary and I have trusted you for years with my deepest secrets... sorry, but some things are best left unsaid...

It's ya girl,
Chloe Baguette Carter

P.S. No longer Mrs. Wright

The aftermath...

Brezell sat in the prison's infirmary fuming at humanity. For some reason or another, he felt like the world owed him something. He grunted loudly as the nurse cleaned his wounds and changed his shit bag. He contemplated returning to his cell and opening several letters he'd received from Chloe. The last few months, he threw all of his mail in a garbage bag. He still had a strong hatred for her and planned to seek revenge, even if he did have to wait thirty years or more. Others on his list included Karma, Komara, Monte, Brea, and BG. The only regrets Brezell had were not killing Chloe and Monte when he had the chance. In his twisted mind, he had done no wrong. He was simply seeking vengeance for his mother's death. He felt no remorse and refuse to apologize for any of his actions.

He often repeated to himself daily, *"No walls can hold me forever."* He planned to carry out his fatality task if he died trying.

"Thanks for taking good care of me, gorgeous." Brezell thanked and complimented the young nurse. Blushing from ear-to-ear, she'd waited years to encounter the man she had a huge crush on back in school.

"Damn, even on your worst day, your still fine as ever and hung like a damn camel," she whispered in his ear.

"Where do I know you from again?" he questioned pretending not to remember.

"Bloom High School," she gleamed at the attention he was giving her.

Brezell gently rubbed the nurse's thigh. When she didn't reject, he knew he had his next victim and new strong connection to the outside world.

I'll be outta this bitch in no time. I'm coming for you muthafuckas, you betta watch the fuck out! When one door closes, another opens, shit don't stop, he reflected to himself.

In a few months, his colostomy bag was to be removed and from then, it was on.

Brezell laid back with his hands behind his head and smiled his sinister smile.

It's on bitches. Just give me six months to plan my shit right.

Diary of a Kingpin's Daughter

PTE Order Form

QTY	TITLE	PRICE
	Around The Way Girls 2 by KaShamba Williams, LaJill Hunt & Thomas Long	$14.95
	At The Courts Mercy by KaShamba Williams	$14.95
	No Good Dirty Dawg by Unique J. Shannon	$14.95
	Allegheny Doe Boy by G. Rell	$14.95
	Dialing For Pain by KaShamba Williams	$14.95
	DRIVEN by KaShamba Williams	$14.95
	Girls From Da Hood 2 by K. Williams, Nikki Turner & Joy	$14.95
	Girls From Da Hood 3 by K.Williams, Mark Anthony, Madame K	$14.95
	Hittin' Numbers by Unique J. Shannon	$14.95
	In My Peace I Trust by Brittney Davis	$14.95
	It's Like Butta, Baby by Caramel	$14.95
	Latin Heat by BP Love	$14.95
	One Love 'Til I Die by Tony Trusell	$14.95
	Mind Games by KaShamba Williams	$14.95
	Stiletto 101 by Lenaise Meyeil	$14.95
	Thug's Passion by Tracy Gray	$14.95
	Even Sinners Have Souls	$14.95
	PLATINUM TEEN SERIES	
	Dymond In The Rough	$6.99
	The AB-solute Truth	$6.99
	Runaway	$6.99
	Best Kept Secret	$6.99
	Total:	

Please include shipping and handling fee of $2.50.
Forms of payment accepted – money orders, credit card,
Paypal, debit cards, postal stamps, and Institutional checks.
Please allow 5-7 business days for books to ship Media Mail.

Precioustymes Entertainment
229 Governors Place, #138
Bear, DE 19701

New Titles

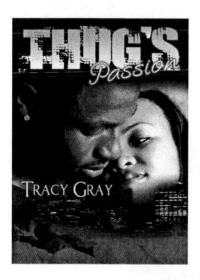

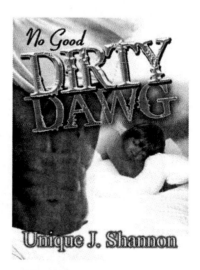

Searching for "safe" Urban Fiction books for your
10-15 year olds to read?
Try the Platinum Teen Series.
No explicit language or explicit content.

PTE is the 1st Urban Fiction Publishing
Company to delivery a teen series of this kind!!

Diary of a Kingpin's Daughter

PTE Order Form

QTY	TITLE	PRICE
	Around The Way Girls 2 by KaShamba Williams, LaJill Hunt & Thomas Long	$14.95
	At The Courts Mercy by KaShamba Williams	$14.95
	No Good Dirty Dawg by Unique J. Shannon	$14.95
	Allegheny Doe Boy by G. Rell	$14.95
	Dialing For Pain by KaShamba Williams	$14.95
	DRIVEN by KaShamba Williams	$14.95
	Girls From Da Hood 2 by K. Williams, Nikki Turner & Joy	$14.95
	Girls From Da Hood 3 by K.Williams, Mark Anthony, Madame K	$14.95
	Hittin' Numbers by Unique J. Shannon	$14.95
	In My Peace I Trust by Brittney Davis	$14.95
	It's Like Butta, Baby by Caramel	$14.95
	Latin Heat by BP Love	$14.95
	One Love 'Til I Die by Tony Trusell	$14.95
	Mind Games by KaShamba Williams	$14.95
	Stiletto 101 by Lenaise Meyeil	$14.95
	Thug's Passion by Tracy Gray	$14.95
	Even Sinners Have Souls	$14.95
	PLATINUM TEEN SERIES	
	Dymond In The Rough	$6.99
	The AB-solute Truth	$6.99
	Runaway	$6.99
	Best Kept Secret	$6.99
	Total:	

Please include shipping and handling fee of $2.50.

In stores now!

By Lenaise Meyeil

April 2008

By Lenaise Meyeil
247

Diary of a Kingpin's Daughter

PTE Order Form

QTY	TITLE	PRICE
	Around The Way Girls 2 by KaShamba Williams, LaJill Hunt & Thomas Long	$14.95
	At The Courts Mercy by KaShamba Williams	$14.95
	No Good Dirty Dawg by Unique J. Shannon	$14.95
	Allegheny Doe Boy by G. Rell	$14.95
	Dialing For Pain by KaShamba Williams	$14.95
	DRIVEN by KaShamba Williams	$14.95
	Girls From Da Hood 2 by K. Williams, Nikki Turner & Joy	$14.95
	Girls From Da Hood 3 by K.Williams, Mark Anthony, Madame K	$14.95
	Hittin' Numbers by Unique J. Shannon	$14.95
	In My Peace I Trust by Brittney Davis	$14.95
	It's Like Butta, Baby by Caramel	$14.95
	Latin Heat by BP Love	$14.95
	One Love 'Til I Die by Tony Trusell	$14.95
	Mind Games by KaShamba Williams	$14.95
	Stiletto 101 by Lenaise Meyeil	$14.95
	Thug's Passion by Tracy Gray	$14.95
	Even Sinners Have Souls	$14.95
	PLATINUM TEEN SERIES	
	Dymond In The Rough	$6.99
	The AB-solute Truth	$6.99
	Runaway	$6.99
	Best Kept Secret	$6.99
	Total:	

THIS IS NOT A GAME!

~Times are precious, never waste it on negativity~

RELEASED IN JAPAN

WWW.KASHAMBAWILLIAMS.COM

www.precioustymes.com

www.myspace.com/precioustymesent

229 Governors Place, #138
Bear, DE 19701

By Lenaise Meyeil

Black & Nobel Books
&
Distribution

1411 W. Erie Avenue
Philadelphia, PA
(215) 965-1559

www.myspace.com/blackandnobelbooks
www.blackandnobel.com

By Lenaise Meyeil

Diary of a Kingpin's Daughter

NOW AVAILABLE AT PTE

RJ Publications

QTY	TITLE	PRICE
	Blood of My Brother by Zoe & Yusuf Woods	$14.95
	Chasin' Satisfaction by W.S. Burkett	$14.95
	Extreme Circumstances by Cereka Cook	$14.95
	Me and Mrs. Jones by K.M. Thompson	$14.95
	Neglected Souls by Richard Jeanty	$14.95
	Neglected No More by Richard Jeanty	$14.95
	Sexual Exploits of a Nympho by R. Jeanty	$14.95
	Sexual Exploits of a Nympho Part II by R.J.	$14.95
	Sexual Jeopardy by Richard Jeanty	$14.95
	Stick and Move by Shawn Black	$14.95
	The Evil Side of Money by Jeff Robertson	$14.95
	The Most Dangerous Gang in America, NYPD by Richard Jeanty	$14.95
	Too Many Secrets, Too Many Lies by Sonya Sparks	$14.95
	Whip Appeal by Richard Jeanty	$14.95
	Total:	

www.rjpublications.com

Please include shipping and handling fee of $2.50.
Forms of payment accepted – money orders, credit card,
Paypal, debit cards, postal stamps, and Institutional checks.
Please allow 5-7 business days for books to ship Media Mail.

Diary of a Kingpin's Daughter

NOW AVAILABLE AT PTE

RJ Publications

QTY	TITLE	PRICE
	Blood of My Brother by Zoe & Yusuf Woods	$14.95
	Chasin' Satisfaction by W.S. Burkett	$14.95
	Extreme Circumstances by Cereka Cook	$14.95
	Me and Mrs. Jones by K.M. Thompson	$14.95
	Neglected Souls by Richard Jeanty	$14.95
	Neglected No More by Richard Jeanty	$14.95
	Sexual Exploits of a Nympho by R. Jeanty	$14.95
	Sexual Exploits of a Nympho Part II by R.J.	$14.95
	Sexual Jeopardy by Richard Jeanty	$14.95
	Stick and Move by Shawn Black	$14.95
	The Evil Side of Money by Jeff Robertson	$14.95
	The Most Dangerous Gang in America, NYPD by Richard Jeanty	$14.95
	Too Many Secrets, Too Many Lies by Sonya Sparks	$14.95
	Whip Appeal by Richard Jeanty	$14.95
	Total:	

www.rjpublications.com

Please include shipping and handling fee of $2.50.
Forms of payment accepted – money orders, credit card,
Paypal, debit cards, postal stamps, and Institutional checks.
Please allow 5-7 business days for books to ship Media Mail.

RJ Publications titles

W.S. BURKETT SONYA SPARKS Zoe & Yusuf T. Woods

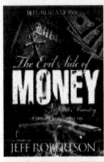

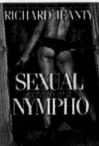

JEFF ROBERTSON RICHARD JEANTY RICHARD JEANTY

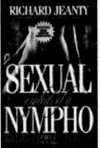

SHAWN BLACK CEREKA COOK K.M. THOMPSON

By Lenaise Meyeil

254

Diary of a Kingpin's Daughter

For all your graphic design needs contact
www.ocjgraphix.com.

FOR MORE INFO CONTACT
etaraska@comcast.net
PH# 856.481.4708

We do it all...banners, signs, posters, brochures, menus, comment cards, thank you cards, flyers and much more!

WE BRING YOUR STORY TO REALITY!!!!
BCDESIGN@OCJGRAPHIX.COM - 302.898.4543

By Lenaise Meyeil